She took a step closer to him. "Hold still."

Wariness leapt into the depths of his brown eyes, but he froze.

He smelled of leather and wood shavings, and hot, sun-warmed male. She brushed her fingers against the blade of his cheekbone, feeling warm, smooth skin.

At her touch their gazes clashed and the wariness in his eyes shifted instantly to something else, and for a moment she forgot what she was doing, her fingers frozen on his skin.

"You, um, had a little bit of sawdust on your cheek. I didn't want it to find its way into your eye."

"Thanks." She wasn't sure if it was her imagination or not but his voice sounded decidedly hoarse.

She forced a smile and stepped back, though what she really wanted to do was wrap her arms fiercely around his warm, strong neck and hold on for dear life.

"You're welcome," she managed.

Dear Reader,

I was so excited to write the story of Julia Blair and Will Garrett. From the moment these two characters appeared in my head, while I was coming up with the idea for the trilogy that became THE WOMEN OF BRAMBLEBERRY HOUSE, Julia and Will seemed like dear friends. I cared about them from the very beginning and couldn't wait to explore their journey toward finding each other again.

This reunion story seemed particularly sweet to me—two lost and hurting souls who rediscover the innocence and joy of first love and come to care deeply for each other as adults.

I must admit that as a writer I dislike having to send my characters crawling through some of the painful situations I create. Just as some part of me wants to protect my own children from anything bad that comes along in real life, I hate to make my heroes and heroines suffer.

But I have always felt the job of parents is to provide their children with the tools they need to face hard times, to prepare them so they don't bend and break in the inevitable storms that are a part of life. I suppose it's the same with my heroes and heroines. I am always heartened by the courage my characters—and my children—find to overcome all obstacles. I learn great lessons from each of them!

All my best,

RaeAnne

HIS SECOND-CHANCE FAMILY

RAEANNE THAYNE

SPECIAL EDITION

Published by Silhouette Books

America's Publisher of Contemporary Romance

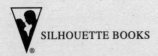

SILHOUETTE BOOKS

ISBN-13: 978-0-373-24874-2
ISBN-10:   0-373-24874-1

HIS SECOND-CHANCE FAMILY

Books by RaeAnne Thayne

Silhouette Special Edition

††*Light the Stars* #1748
††*Dancing in the Moonlight* #1755
††*Dalton's Undoing* #1764
***The Daddy Makeover* #1857
***His Second-Chance Family* #1874

Silhouette Romantic Suspense

The Wrangler and the Runaway Mom #960
Saving Grace #995
Renegade Father #1062
**The Valentine Two-Step* #1133
**Taming Jesse James* #1139
**Cassidy Harte and the Comeback Kid* #1144
The Quiet Storm #1218
Freefall #1239
Nowhere To Hide #1264
†*Nothing To Lose* #1321
†*Never Too Late* #1364
The Interpreter #1380
High-Risk Affair #1448
Shelter from the Storm #1467
High-Stakes Honeymoon #1475

*Outlaw Hartes
†The Searchers
**The Women of Brambleberry House
††The Cowboys of Cold Creek

RAEANNE THAYNE

finds inspiration in the beautiful northern Utah mountains, where she lives with her husband and three children. Her books have won numerous honors, including a RITA® Award nomination from Romance Writers of America and a Career Achievement Award from *Romantic Times BOOKreviews* magazine. RaeAnne loves to hear from readers and can be reached through her Web site at www.raeannethayne.com or at P.O. Box 6682, North Logan, UT 84341.

For the staff and donors of
The Sunshine Foundation, for five days of
unimaginable joy. Sometimes wishes do come true!

Chapter One

As signs from heaven went, this one seemed fairly prosaic.

No choir of angels, no booming voice from above or anything like that. It was simply a hand-lettered placard shoved into the seagrass in front of the massive, ornate Victorian that had drifted through her memory for most of her life.

Apartment For Rent.

Julia stared at the sign with growing excitement. It seemed impossible, a miracle. That *this* house, of all places, would be available for rent just as she was looking for a temporary home seemed just the encouragement her doubting heart needed to reaffirm her decision to pack up her twins and take a new teaching job in Cannon Beach.

Not even to herself had she truly admitted how worried she was that she'd made a terrible mistake moving here, leaving everything familiar and heading into the unknown.

Seeing that sign in front of Brambleberry House seemed an answer to prayer, a confirmation that this was where she and her little family were supposed to be.

"Cool house!" Maddie exclaimed softly, gazing up in awe at the three stories of Queen Anne Victorian, with its elaborate trim, cupolas and weathered shake roof. "It looks like a gingerbread house!"

Julia squeezed her daughter's hand, certain Maddie looked a little healthier today in the bracing sea air of the Oregon Coast.

"Cool dog!" Her twin, Simon, yelled. The words were barely out of his mouth when a giant red blur leaped over the low wrought-iron fence surrounding the house and wriggled around them with glee, as if he'd been waiting years just for them to walk down the beach.

The dog licked Simon's face and headbutted his stomach like an old friend. Julia braced herself to push him away if he got too rough with Maddie, but she needn't have worried. As if guided by some sixth sense, the dog stopped his wild gyrations and waited docilely for Maddie to reach out a tentative hand and pet him. Maddie giggled, a sound that was priceless as all the sea glass in the world to Julia.

"I think he likes me," she whispered.

"I think so, too, sweetheart." Julia smiled and tucked a strand of Maddie's fine short hair behind her ear.

"Do you really know the lady who lives here?" Maddie asked, while Simon was busy wrestling the dog in the sand.

"I used to, a long, long time ago," Julia answered. "She was my very best friend."

Her heart warmed as she remembered Abigail Dandridge and her unfailing kindness to a lonely little girl. Her mind filled with memories of admiring her vast doll collection, of pruning the rose hedge along the fence with her, of shared confidences and tea parties and sand dollar hunts along the beach.

"Like Jenna back home is my best friend?" Maddie asked.

"That's right."

Every summer of her childhood, Brambleberry House became a haven of serenity and peace for her. Her family rented the same cottage just down the beach each July. It should have been a time of rest and enjoyment, but her parents couldn't stop fighting even on vacation.

Whenever she managed to escape to Abigail and Brambleberry House, though, Julia didn't have to listen to their arguments, didn't have to see her mother's tears or her father's obvious impatience at the enforced holiday, his wandering eye.

Her fifteenth summer was the last time she'd been

here. Her parents finally divorced, much to her and her older brother Charlie's relief, and they never returned to Cannon Beach. But over the years, she had used the image of this house, with its soaring gables and turrets, and the peace she had known here to help center her during difficult times.

Through her parents' bitter divorce, through her own separation from Kevin and worse. Much worse.

"Is she still your best friend?" Maddie asked.

"I haven't seen Miss Abigail for many, many years," she said. "But you know, I don't think I realized until just this moment how very much I've missed her."

She should never have let so much time pass before coming back to Cannon Beach. She had let their friendship slip away, too busy being a confused and rebellious teenager caught in the middle of the endless drama between her parents. And then had come college and marriage and family.

Perhaps now that she was back, they could find that friendship once more. She couldn't wait to find out.

She opened the wrought-iron gate and headed up the walkway feeling as if she were on the verge of something oddly portentous.

She rang the doorbell and heard it echo through the house. Anticipation zinged through her as she waited, wondering what she would possibly say to Abigail after all these years. Would her lovely, wrinkled features match Julia's memory?

No one answered after several moments, even after she rang the doorbell a second time. She stood on the porch, wondering if she ought to leave a note with their hotel and her cell phone number, but it seemed impersonal, somehow, after all these years.

They would just have to check back, she decided. She headed back down the stairs and started for the gate again just as she heard the whine of a power tool from behind the house.

The dog, who looked like a mix between an Irish setter and a golden retriever, barked and headed toward the sound, pausing at the corner of the house, head cocked, as if waiting for them to come along with him.

After a wary moment, she followed, Maddie and Simon close on her heels.

The dog led them to the backyard, where Julia found a couple of sawhorses set up and a man with brown hair and broad shoulders running a circular saw through a board.

She watched for a moment, waiting for their presence to attract his attention, but he didn't look up from his work.

"Hello," she called out. When he still didn't respond, she moved closer so she would be in his field of vision and waved.

"Excuse me!"

Finally, he shut off the saw and pulled his safety goggles off, setting them atop his head.

"Yeah?" he said.

She squinted and looked closer at him. He looked

familiar. A hint of a memory danced across her subconscious and she was so busy trying to place him that it took her a moment to respond.

"I'm sorry to disturb you. I rang the doorbell but I guess you couldn't hear me back here with the power tools."

"Guess not."

He spoke tersely, as if impatient to return to work, and Julia could feel herself growing flustered. She had braced herself to see Abigail, not some solemn-eyed construction worker in a sexy tool belt.

"I…right. Um, I'm looking for Abigail Dandridge."

There was an awkward pause and she thought she saw something flicker in his blue eyes.

"Are you a friend of hers?" he asked, his voice not quite as abrupt as it had been before.

"I used to be, a long time ago. Can you tell me when she'll be back? I don't mind waiting."

The dog barked, only with none of the exuberance he had shown a few moments ago, almost more of a whine than a bark. He plopped onto the grass and dipped his chin to his front paws, his eyes suddenly morose.

The man gazed at the dog's curious behavior for a moment. A muscle tightened in his jaw then he looked back at Julia. "Abigail died in April. Heart attack in her sleep. I'm sorry to be the one to tell you."

Julia couldn't help her instinctive cry of distress. Even through her sudden surge of grief, she sensed when Maddie stepped closer and slipped a small, frail hand in hers.

Julia drew a breath, then another. "I...see," she mumbled.

Just one more loss in a long, unrelenting string, she thought. But this one seemed to pierce her heart like jagged driftwood.

It was silly, really, when she thought about it. Abigail hadn't been a presence in her life for sixteen years, but suddenly the loss of her seemed overwhelming.

She swallowed hard, struggling for composure. Her friend was gone, but her house was still here, solid and reassuring, weathering this storm as it had others for generations.

Somehow it seemed more important than ever that she bring her children here.

"I see," she repeated, more briskly now, though she thought she saw a surprising understanding in the deep blue of the man's eyes, so disconcertingly familiar. She knew him. She knew she did.

"I suppose I should talk to you, then. The sign out front says there's an apartment for rent. How many bedrooms does it have?"

He gave her a long look before turning away to pick up another board and carry it to the saw. "Three bedrooms, two of them on the small side. Kitchen's been redone in the last few months and the electricity's been upgraded but the bathroom plumbing's still in pretty rough shape."

"I don't care about that, as long as everything works okay. Three bedrooms is exactly the size my children and I need. Is it still available?'

"Can't say."

She pursed her lips. "Why not?"

He shrugged. "I don't own the place. I live a few houses down the beach. I'm just doing some repairs for the owners."

Something about what he said jarred loose a flood of memories and she stared at him more closely. Suddenly everything clicked in and she gasped, stunned she hadn't realized his identity the instant she had clapped eyes on him.

"Will? Will Garrett?"

He peered at her. "Do I know you?"

She managed a smile. "Probably not. It's been years."

She held out a hand, her pulse suddenly wild and erratic, as it had always been around him.

"Julia Blair. You knew me when I was Julia Hudson. My parents rented a cottage between your house and Brambleberry House every summer of my childhood until I was fifteen. I used to follow you and my older brother Charlie around everywhere."

Will Garrett. She'd forgotten so much about those summers, but never him. She had wondered whether she would see him, had wondered about his life and where he might end up. She never expected to find him standing in front of her on her first full day in town.

"It's been years!" she repeated. "I can't believe you're still here."

At her words, it took Will all of about two seconds to remember her. When he did, he couldn't understand why he hadn't seen it before. He had yearned for Julia Hudson that summer as only a relatively innocent sixteen-year-old boy can ache. He had dreamed of her green eyes and her dimples and her soft, burgeoning curves.

She had been his first real love and had haunted his dreams.

She had promised to keep in touch but she hadn't called or answered any of his letters and he remembered how his teenage heart had been shattered. But by the time school started a month later, he'd been so busy with football practice and school and working for his dad's carpentry business on Saturdays that he hadn't really had much time to wallow in his heartbreak.

Julia looked the same—the same smile, the same auburn hair, the same appealing dimples—while he felt as if he had aged a hundred years.

He could barely remember those innocent, carefree days when he had been certain the world was his for the taking, that he could achieve anything if only he worked hard enough for it.

She was waiting for a response, he realized, still

holding her hand outstretched in pleased welcome. He held up his hands in their leather work gloves as an excuse not to touch her. After an awkward moment, she dropped her arms to her side, though the smile remained fixed on her lovely features.

"I can't believe you're still here in Cannon Beach," she repeated. "How wonderful that you've stayed all these years! I remember how you loved it here."

He wouldn't call it wonderful. There were days he felt like some kind of prehistoric iceman, frozen forever in place. He had wondered for some time if he ought to pick up and leave, go *anywhere*, just as long as it wasn't here.

Someone with his carpentry skills and experience could find work just about any place. He had thought about it long and hard, especially at night when the memories overwhelmed him and the emptiness seemed to ring through his house but he couldn't seem to work past the inertia to make himself leave.

"So how have you been?" Julia asked. "What about family? Are you married? Any kids?"

Okay, he wasn't a prehistoric iceman. He was pretty certain they couldn't bleed and bleed and bleed.

He set his jaw and picked up the oak board he was shaping for a new window frame in one of the third-floor bedrooms of Brambleberry House.

"You'll have to talk to Sage Benedetto or Anna Galvez about the apartment," he said tersely. "They're the new owners. They should be back this evening."

He didn't quite go so far as to fire up the circular saw

but it was a clear dismissal, rude as hell. He had to hope she got the message that he wasn't interested in any merry little trips down memory lane.

She gave him a long, measuring look while the girl beside her edged closer.

After a moment, she offered a smile that was cool and polite but still managed to scorch his conscience. "I'll do that. Thank you. It's good to see you again, Will."

He nodded tersely. This time, he did turn on the circular saw, though he was aware of every move she and her children made in the next few moments. He knew just when they walked around the house with Abigail's clever Irish Setter mix Conan following on their heels.

He gave up any pretense of working when he saw them head across the lane out front, then head down the beach. She still walked with grace and poise, her chin up as if ready to take on the world, just as she had when she was fifteen years old.

And her kids. That curious boy and the fragile-looking girl with the huge, luminescent blue eyes. Remembering those eyes, he had to set down the board and press a hand to the dull ache in his chest, though he knew from two years' experience nothing would ease it.

Booze could dull it for a moment but not nearly long enough. When the alcohol wore off, everything rushed back, worse than before.

He was still watching their slow, playful progress down the beach when Conan returned to the backyard.

The dog barked once and gave him a look Will could only describe as peeved. He planted his haunches in front of the worktable and glared at him.

Abigail would have given him exactly the same look for treating an old friend with such rudeness.

"Yeah, I was a jerk," he muttered. "She caught me off guard, that's all. I wasn't exactly prepared for a ghost from the past to show up out of the blue this afternoon."

The dog barked again and Will wondered, not for the first time, what went on inside his furry head. Conan had a weird way of looking at everybody as if he knew exactly what they might be thinking and he managed to communicate whole diatribes with only a bark and a certain expression in his doleful eyes.

Abigail had loved the dog. For that reason alone, Will would have tolerated him since his neighbor had been one of his favorite people on earth. But Conan had also showed an uncanny knack over the last two years for knowing just when Will was at low ebb.

More than once, there had been times when he had been out on the beach wondering if it would be easier just to walk out into the icy embrace of the tide than to survive another second of this unrelenting grief.

No matter the time of day or night, Conan would somehow always show up, lean against Will's legs until the despair eased, and then would follow him home before returning to Brambleberry House and Abigail.

He sighed now as the dog continued to wordlessly

reprimand him. "What do you want me to do? Go after her?"

Conan barked and Will shook his head. "No way. Forget it."

He *should* go after her, at least to apologize. He had been unforgivably rude. The hell of it was, he didn't really know why. He wasn't cold by nature. Through the last two years, he had tried to hold to the hard-fought philosophy that just because his insides had been ripped apart and because sometimes the grief and pain seemed to crush the life out of him, he hadn't automatically been handed a free pass to hurt others.

Lashing out at others around him did nothing to ease his own pain so he made it a point to be polite to just about everybody.

Sure, there were random moments when his bleakness slipped through. At times, Sage and Anna and other friends had been upset at him when he pushed away their efforts to comfort him. More than a few times, truth be told. But he figured it was better to be by himself during those dark moments than to do as he'd just done, lash out simply because he didn't know how else to cope.

He had no excuse for treating her poorly. He had just seen her there looking so lovely and bright with her energetic son and her pretty little daughter and every muscle inside him had cramped in pain.

The children set it off. He could see that now. The girl had even looked a little like Cara—same coloring, anyway, though Cara had been chubby and round where Julia's daughter looked as if she might blow away in anything more than a two-knot wind.

It hadn't only been the children, though. He had seen Julia standing there in a shaft of sunlight and for a moment, long-dormant feelings had stirred inside him that he wanted to stay dead and buried like the rest of his life.

No matter how screwed up he was, he had no business being rude to her and her children. Like it or not, he would have to apologize to her, especially if Anna and Sage rented her the apartment.

He lived three houses away and spent a considerable amount of time at Brambleberry House, both because he was busy with various remodeling projects and because he considered the new owners—Abigail's heirs—his friends.

He didn't want Julia Hudson Blair or her children here at Brambleberry House. If he were honest with himself, he could admit that he would have preferred if she had stayed a long-buried memory.

But she hadn't. She was back in Cannon Beach with her children, looking to rent an apartment at Brambleberry House, so apparently she planned to stay at least awhile.

Chances were good he would bump into her again, so he was going to have to figure out a way to apologize.

He watched their shapes grow smaller and smaller as

they walked down the beach toward town and he rubbed the ache in his chest, wondering what it would take to convince Sage and Anna to find a different tenant.

Chapter Two

"Will we get to see inside the pretty house this time, Mommy?"

Julia lifted her gaze from the road for only an instant to glance in the rearview mirror of her little Toyota SUV. Even from here, she could see the excitement in Maddie's eyes and she couldn't help but smile in return at her daughter.

"That's the plan," she answered, turning her attention back to the road as she drove past a spectacular hotel set away from the road. Someday when she was independently wealthy with unlimited leisure time, she wanted to stay at The Sea Urchin, one of the most exclusive boutique hotels on the coast.

"I talked to one of the owners of the house an hour ago," Julia continued, "and she invited us to walk through and see if the apartment will work for us,"

"I hope it does," Simon said. "I really liked that cool dog."

"I'm not sure the dog lives there," she answered. "He might belong to the man we talked to this morning. Will Garrett. He doesn't live there, he was just doing some work on the house."

"I'm glad he doesn't live there," Maddie said in her whisper-soft voice. "He was kind of cranky."

Julia agreed, though she didn't say as much to her children. Will had been terse, bordering on rude, and for the life of her she couldn't figure out why. What had she done? She hadn't seen him in sixteen years. It seemed ridiculous to assume he might be angry, after all these years, simply because she hadn't written to him as she had promised.

They had been friends of a sort—and more than friends for a few glorious weeks one summer. She remembered moonlight bonfires and holding hands in the movies and stealing kisses on the beach.

She would have assumed their shared past warranted at least a little politeness but apparently he didn't agree. The Will Garrett she remembered had been far different from the surly stranger they met that afternoon. She couldn't help wondering if he treated everyone that way or if she received special treatment.

"He was simply busy," she said now to her children. "We interrupted his work and I think he was eager to get back to it. We grown-ups can sometimes be impatient."

"I remember," Simon said. "Dad was like that sometimes."

The mention of Kevin took her by surprise. Neither twin referred to their father very often anymore. He had died more than two years ago and had been a distant presence for some time before that, and they had all walked what felt like a million miles since then.

Brambleberry House suddenly came into view, rising above the fringy pines and spruce trees. She slowed, savoring the sight of the spectacular Victorian mansion silhouetted against the salmon-colored sky, with the murky blue sea below.

That familiar sense of homecoming washed over her again as she pulled into the pebbled driveway. She wanted to live here with her children. To wake up in the morning with that view of the sea out her window and the smell of roses drifting up from the gardens and the solid comfort of those walls around her.

As she pulled into the driveway and turned off the engine, she gave a silent prayer that she and the twins would click with the new owners. The one she'd spoken with earlier—Sage Benedetto—had seemed cordial when she invited Julia and her children to take a look at the apartment, but Julia was almost afraid to hope.

"Mom, look!" Simon exclaimed. "There's the dog! Does that mean he lives here?"

As she opened her door to climb out, she saw the big shaggy red dog waiting by the wrought-iron gates, almost as if he somehow knew they were on their way.

"I don't know. We'll have to see."

"Oh, I hope so." Maddie pushed a wisp of hair out of her eyes. She looked fragile and pale. Though Julia would have liked to walk from their hotel downtown to enjoy the spectacular views of Cannon Beach at sunset, she had been afraid Maddie wouldn't have the strength for another long hike down the beach and back.

Now she was grateful she had heeded her motherly instincts that seemed to have become superacute since Maddie's illness.

More than anything—more than she wanted to live in this house, more than she wanted this move to work out, more than she wanted to *breathe*—she wanted her daughter to be healthy and strong.

"I hope we can live here," Maddie said. "I really like that dog."

Julia hugged her daughter and helped her out of her seatbelt. Maddie slipped a hand in hers while Simon took his sister's other hand. Together, the three of them walked through the gate, where the one-dog welcoming committee awaited them.

The dog greeted Simon with the same enthusiasm he had shown that morning, wagging his tail fiercely and nudging Simon's hand with his head. After a moment of attention from her son, the dog turned to Maddie. Julia went on full mother-bear alert, again ready to step in if necessary, but the dog showed the same uncanny gentleness to Maddie.

He simply planted his haunches on the sidewalk in front of her, waiting as still as one of those cheap plaster dog statues for Maddie to reach out with a giggle and pet his head.

Weird, she thought, but she didn't have time to figure it out before the front door opened. A woman wearing shorts and a brightly colored tank top stepped out onto the porch. She looked to be in her late twenties and was extraordinarily lovely in an exotic kind of way, with blonde wavy hair pulled back in a ponytail and an olive complexion that spoke of a Mediterranean heritage.

She walked toward them with a loose-hipped gait and a warm smile.

"Hi!" Her voice held an open friendliness and Julia instinctively responded to it. She could feel the tension in her shoulders relax a little as the other woman held out a hand.

"I'm Sage Benedetto. You must be the Blairs."

She shook it. "Yes. I'm Julia and these are my children, Simon and Maddie."

Sage dropped her hand and turned to the twins. "Hey kids. Great to meet you! How old are you? Let me guess. Sixteen?"

They both giggled. "No!" Simon exclaimed. "We're seven."

"Seven? Both of you?"

"We're twins." Maddie said in her soft voice.

"Twins? No kidding? Cool! I've always wanted to have a twin. You ever dress up in each others' clothes and try to trick your mom?"

"No!" Maddie said with another giggle.

"We're not *identical* twins," Simon said with a roll of his eyes. "We're *fraternal.*"

"Of course you are. Silly me. 'Cause one of you is a boy and one is a girl, right?"

Sage obviously knew her way around children, Julia thought as she listened to their exchange. That was definitely a good sign. She had observed during her career as an elementary school teacher that many adults didn't really know how to talk to kids. They either tried too hard to be buddies or treated them with obvious condescension. Sage managed to find the perfect middle ground.

"I see you've met Conan," Sage said, scratching the big dog under the chin.

"Is he your dog?" Simon asked.

She smiled at the animal with obvious affection. "I guess you could say that. Or I'm his human. Either way, we kind of look out for each other, don't we, bud?"

Oddly, Julia could swear the dog grinned.

"Thank you again for agreeing to show the apartment to us tonight," she said.

Sage turned her smile to Julia. "No problem. I'm sorry we weren't here when you came by the first time. You said on the telephone that you knew Abigail."

That pang of loss pinched at her again as she imagined Abigail out here in the garden, her big floppy straw hat and her gardening gloves and the tray of lemonade always waiting on the porch.

"Years ago," she answered, then was compelled to elaborate.

"Every summer my family rented a house near here. The year I was ten, my brother and I were running around on the beach and I cut my foot on a broken shell. Abigail heard me crying and came down to help. She brought me back up to the house, fixed me a cookie and doctored me up. We were fast friends after that. Every year, I would run up here the minute we pulled into the driveway of our cottage. Abigail always seemed so happy to see me and we would get along as if I had never left."

The other woman smiled, though there was an edge of sorrow to it. Julia wondered again how Sage had ended up as one of the two new owners of Brambleberry House after Abigail's death.

"Sounds just like Abigail," Sage said. "She made friends with everyone she met."

"I've been terrible about keeping in contact with her," Julia admitted with chagrin as they walked into the entryway of the house, with its sweeping staircase and polished honey oak trim. "I was so sorry to hear about her death—more sorry than I can say that I let so much time go by without calling her. I suppose some foolish part of me just assumed she would always be here. Like the ocean and the seastacks."

The dog—Conan—whined a little, almost as if he understood their conversation, though Julia knew that was impossible.

"I think we all felt that way," Sage said. "It's been four months and it still doesn't seem real."

"Will said she died of a heart attack in her sleep."

"That's right. I find some comfort in knowing that if she could have chosen her exit scene, that's exactly how she would have wanted to go. The doctors said she probably slept right through it."

Sage paused and gave her a considering kind of look. "Do you know Will, then?"

Julia could feel color climb her cheekbones. How foolish could she be to blush over a teenage crush on Will Garrett, when the man he had become obviously wanted nothing to do with her?

"Knew him," she corrected. "It all seems so long ago. The cottage we rented every year was next door to his. We socialized a little with his family and he and my older brother Charlie were friends. I usually tried to find a way to tag along, to their great annoyance."

She had a sudden memory of mountain biking through the mists and primordial green of Ecola

National Park, then cooling off in the frigid surf of Indian Beach, the gulls wheeling overhead and the ocean song a sweet accompaniment.

Will had kissed her for the first time there, while her brother was busy body surfing through the baby breakers and not paying them any attention. It had just been a quick, furtive brush of his lips, but she could suddenly remember with vivid clarity how it had warmed her until she forgot all about the icy swells.

"He was my first love," she confessed.

Oh no. Had she really said that out loud? She wanted to snatch the words back but they hung between them. Sage turned around, sudden speculation sparking in her exotic, tilted eyes, and Julia could feel herself blushing harder.

"Is that right?"

"A long time ago," she answered, though she was certain she had said those words about a million times already. So much for making a good impression. She was stuttering and blushing and acting like an idiot over a man who barely remembered her.

To her relief, Sage didn't pursue it as they reached the second floor of the big house.

"This is the apartment we're renting. It's been vacant most of the time in the five years I've lived here. Once in a while Abigail opened it up on a short-term basis to various people in need of a comfortable place to crash for a while. Since Anna and I inherited Brambleberry

House, we've kept Will busy fixing it up so we could rent out the space."

Will again. Couldn't she escape him for three seconds? "Convenient that he lives close," she said.

"It's more convenient because he's the best carpenter around. With all the work that needs to be done to Brambleberry House, we could hire him as our resident carpenter. Good thing for us he likes to stay busy."

She remembered again the pain in his eyes. She wanted to ask Sage the reason for it, but she knew that would be far too presumptuous.

Anyway, she wasn't here to talk about Will Garrett. She was trying to find a clean, comfortable place for her children.

When Sage opened the door to the apartment, Julia felt a little thrill of anticipation.

"Ready to take a look?" Sage asked.

"Absolutely." She walked through the door with the oddest sense of homecoming.

The apartment met all her expectations and more. Much, much more. She walked from room to room with a growing excitement. The kitchen was small but had new appliances and what looked like new cabinets stained a lovely cherry color. Each of the three bedrooms had fresh coats of paint. Though two of them were quite small, nearly every room had a breathtaking view of the ocean.

"It's beautiful," she exclaimed as she stood in the

large living room, with its wide windows on two sides that overlooked the sea.

"Will did a good job, didn't he?" Sage said.

Before Julia could answer, the children came into the room, followed by the dog.

"Wow. This place is so cool!" Simon exclaimed.

"I like it, too," Maddie said. "It feels friendly."

"How can a house feel friendly?" her brother scoffed. "It's just walls and a roof and stuff."

Sage didn't seem to mind Maddie's whimsy. Her features softened and she laid a hand on Maddie's hair with a gentleness that warmed Julia's heart.

"I think you're absolutely right, Miss Maddie," she answered. "I've always thought Brambleberry House was just about the friendliest house I've ever been lucky enough to live in."

Maddie smiled back and Julia could see a bond forming between the two of them, just as the children already seemed to have a connection with Conan.

"When can we move in?" Simon asked.

Julia winced at her son's bluntness. "We've still got some details to work out," she said quickly, stepping in to avoid Sage feeling any sense of obligation to answer before she was completely comfortable with the idea of them as tenants. "Nothing's settled yet. Why don't the two of you play with Conan for a few moments while I talk with Ms. Benedetto?"

He seemed satisfied with that and headed to the

window seat, followed closely by his sister and Sage's friendly dog.

Her children were remarkably adept at entertaining themselves. Little wonder, she thought with that echo of sadness. They had spent three years developing patience during Maddie's endless string of appointments and procedures.

When they seemed happily settled petting the dog, she turned back to Sage. "I'm sorry about that. I understand that you need to check references and everything and talk to the co-owner before you make a decision. I'm definitely interested, at least through the school year."

Sage opened her mouth to answer but before she could speak, the dog gave a sudden sharp bark, his ears on alert. He rushed for the open door to the landing and she could hear his claws scrabbling on the steps just an instant before the front door opened downstairs.

Sage didn't even blink at the dog's eager behavior. "Oh, good. That's Anna Galvez. I was hoping she'd be home before you left so she could have a chance to meet you. Anna took over By-the-Wind, Abigail's old book and giftshop in town."

"I remember the place. I spent many wonderful rainy afternoons curled up in one of the easy chairs with a book."

"Haven't we all?" Sage said with a smile, then walked out to the stairs to call down to the other woman.

A moment later, a woman with dark hair and petite,

lovely features walked up the stairs, her hand on Conan's fur.

She greeted Julia with a smile slightly more reserved than Sage's warm friendliness. "Hello."

Her smile warmed when she greeted the curious twins. "Hey, there," she said.

Sage performed a quick introduction. "Julia and her twins are moving to Cannon Beach from Boise. Julia's going to be teaching fifth grade at the elementary school and she's looking for an apartment."

"Lovely to meet you. Welcome to Oregon!"

"Thank you," Julia said. "I used to spend summers near here when I was a child."

"She's one of Abigail's lost sheep finally come home," Sage said with a smile that quickly turned mischievous. "Oh, you'll be interested to know that Will was her first love."

To Julia's immense relief, Sage added the latter in an undertone too low for the children to hear, even if they'd been paying attention. Still, she could feel herself blush again. She really *had* to stop doing that every time Will Garrett's name was mentioned.

"I was fifteen. Another lifetime ago. We barely recognized each other when I bumped into him earlier today outside. He seems…very different than he was at sixteen."

Sage's teasing smile turned sober. "He has his reasons," she said softly.

She and Anna gave each other a quick look loaded with layers of subtext that completely escaped Julia.

"Thank you for showing me the apartment. I have to tell you, from what I see, it would be perfect for us. It's exactly what I'm looking for, with room for the children to play, incredible views and within walking distance to the school. But I certainly understand that you need to check references and credit history before renting it to me. Feel free to talk to the principal of the elementary school who hired me, and any of the other references I gave you in our phone conversation. If you need anything else, you have my cell number and the number of the hotel where we're staying."

"Or we could always talk to Will and see what he remembers from when you were fifteen."

Julia flashed a quick look to Sage and was relieved to find the other woman smiling again. She had no idea what Will Garrett remembered about her. Nothing pleasant, obviously, or he probably would have shown a little more warmth when she encountered him earlier.

"Will may not be the best character reference. If I remember correctly, I still owe him an ice-cream cone. He bet me I couldn't split a geoduck without using my hands. I tried for days but the summer ended before I could pay him back."

"Good thing you're sticking around," Anna said. "You can pay back your debt now. We've still got ice cream."

"And geoducks," Sage said. "Maybe you're more agile than you used to be."

She laughed, liking both women immensely. As she gathered the children and headed down the stairs to her car, Julia could only wish for a little more agility. Then she would cross her toes and her fingers that Sage Benedetto and Anna Galvez would let her and her twins rent their vacant apartment.

She couldn't remember when she had wanted anything so much.

"So what do you think?" Sage asked as she and Anna stood at the window watching the schoolteacher strap her children into the backseat of her little SUV.

She looked like she had the process down to a science, Sage thought, something she still struggled with when she drove Chloe anywhere. She could never figure out how to tighten the darn seat belt over the booster chair with her stepdaughter-to-be. She ought to have Julia give her lessons.

"No idea," Anna replied. "I barely talked to her for five minutes. But she seems nice enough."

"She belongs here."

Anna snorted. "And you figured that out in one quick fifteen-minute meeting?"

"Not at all." Sage grinned. She couldn't help herself. "I figured it out in the first thirty seconds."

"We still have to check her references. I'm sorry if this offends you, but I can't go on karma alone on this one."

"I know. But I'm sure they'll check out." Sage couldn't have said how she knew, she just did. Somehow she was certain Abigail would have wanted Julia and her twins to live at Brambleberry House.

"Did you see her blush when Will's name came up?"

Anna shook her head. "Leave it alone, Sage. You engaged women think you have to match up the entire universe."

"Not the entire universe. Just the people I love, like Will."

And you, she added silently. She thought of the loneliness in Anna's eyes, the tiny shadow of sadness she was certain Anna never guessed showed on her expression.

Their neighbor wasn't the only one who deserved to be happy, but she decided she—and Abigail—could only focus on one thing at a time. "Will has had so much pain in his life. Wouldn't you love to see him smile again?"

"Of course. But Julia herself said she hadn't seen him in years and they barely recognized each other. And we don't even know the woman. She could be married."

"Widowed. She told me that on the phone. Two years, the same as Will."

Compassion flickered in Anna's brown eyes. "Those poor children, to lose their father at such a young age." She paused. "That doesn't mean whatever scheme you're hatching has any chance of working."

"I know. But it's worth a shot. Anyway, Conan likes them and that's the important thing, isn't it, bud?"

The dog barked, giving his uncanny grin. As far as Sage was concerned, references or not, that settled the matter.

Chapter Three

Sage and Anna apparently had a new tenant.

Will slowed his pickup down as he passed Bramble-berry House coming from the south. He couldn't miss the U-Haul trailer hulking in the driveway and he could see Sage heading into the house, her arms stacked high with boxes. Anna was loading her arms with a few more while Julia's children played on the grass not far away with Conan. Even from here he could see the dog's glee at having new playmates.

Damn. This is the price he paid for his inaction. He should have stopped by a day or two earlier and at least tried to dissuade Anna and Sage from taking her on as a tenant.

It probably wouldn't have done any good, he acknowledged. Both of Abigail's heirs could be as stubborn as crooked nails when they had their minds made up about something. Still, he should have at least made the attempt.

But what could he have said, really, that wouldn't have made him sound like a raving lunatic?

Yeah, she seems nice enough and I sure was crazy about her when I was sixteen. But I don't want her around anymore because I don't like being reminded I'm still alive.

He sighed and turned off his truck. He wanted nothing more than to drive past the house and hide out at his place down the beach until she moved on but there was no way on earth his blasted conscience would let him leave three women and two kids to do all that heavy lifting on their own.

He climbed out of his pickup and headed to the trailer. He reached it just as the top box on Anna's stack started to slide.

He lunged for it and plucked the wobbly top box just before it would have hit the ground, earning a surprised look from Anna over the next-highest box.

"Wow! Good catch," she said, a smile lifting her studious features. "Lucky you were here."

"Rule of thumb—your stack of boxes probably shouldn't exceed your own height."

She smiled. "Good advice. I'm afraid I can get a little impatient sometimes."

"Is that it? I thought you just like to bite off more than you can chew."

She made a wry face at him. "That, too. How did you know we needed help?"

He shrugged. "I was driving past and saw your leaning tower and thought you might be able to use another set of arms."

"We've got plenty of arms. We just need some arms with muscle. Thanks for stopping."

"Glad to help." It was a blatant lie but he decided she didn't need to know that.

She turned and headed up the stairs and he grabbed several boxes from inside the truck and followed her, trying to ignore the curious mingle of dread and anticipation in his gut.

He didn't want to see Julia again. He had already dreamed about her the last two nights in a row. More contact would only wedge her more firmly into his head.

At the same time, part of him—maybe the part that was still sixteen years old somewhere deep inside—couldn't help wondering how the years might have changed her.

Anna was breathing hard by the time they reached the middle floor of the house, where the door to the apartment had been propped open with a small stack of books.

"I could have taken another one of your boxes," he said to Anna.

She made a face. "Show-off. Are you even working up a sweat?"

"I'm sweating on the inside," he answered, which was nothing less than the truth.

The source of his trepidation spoke to Anna an instant later.

"Thanks so much," Julia Blair said in her low, sexy voice. "Those go in Simon's bedroom."

Will lowered his boxes so he could see over them and found her standing in the middle of the living room directing traffic. She wore capris and a stretchy yellow T-shirt. With her hair pulled back into a ponytail, she looked fresh and beautiful and not much older than she'd been that last summer together.

He didn't miss the shock in her eyes when she spied him behind the boxes. "Will! What are you doing here?"

He shrugged, uncomfortable at her obvious shock. Why *shouldn't* he be here helping? It was the neighborly thing to do. Had he really been such a complete jerk the other day that she find his small gesture of assistance now so stunning?

"Do these go into the same room?"

She looked flustered, her cheeks slightly pink. "Um, no. Those are my things. They go in my bedroom, the big one overlooking the ocean."

He headed in the direction she pointed, noting again no sign of a Mr. Blair. On some instinctive level, he had subconsciously picked up the fact that she wore no wedding ring when he had seen her the other day and she had spoken only of herself and her children needing an apartment. Was she widowed, divorced, or never married?

He only wondered out of mild curiosity about the road she might have traveled in the years since he had seen her. Or at least that's what he told himself.

In her bedroom, he found stacks of boxes, some of them open and overflowing with books. The queen-size bed was already made up with a cozy-looking comforter in soft blue tones, with piles of pillows against the headboard.

An image flashed in his head of her tousled and welcoming, her auburn hair spread out on those pillows and a soft, aroused smile teasing the edges of those lovely features.

He dropped the boxes so abruptly he barely missed his toe.

Whoa. Where the hell did that come from?

He had no business thinking about her at all, forget about in some kind of sultry, welcoming pose.

When he returned to the living room, her cheeks were still flushed and she didn't meet his gaze, as if she were embarrassed about something. It was a damn good thing she couldn't know the inappropriate direction of his thoughts.

"I'm sorry." She fidgeted with a stack of books in her hand. "I probably sounded terribly ungracious when you first came in. I just didn't expect you to show up and start hauling my boxes inside."

"No problem."

He started to head toward the door, but she apparently wasn't content with his short response. "Why, again, are you helping me move in?"

He shrugged. What did it matter? He was here, wasn't he? Did they really have to analyze the reasons why? "I was heading home after a job south of here and saw your U-Haul out front. I figured you could use a hand."

"How...neighborly of you."

"Around here we look out for each other." It was nothing less than the truth.

"I remember." She smiled a little. "That's one of the reasons I wanted to come back to Cannon Beach. I remembered that sense of community with great affection."

She set the stack of books down on the coffee table, then turned a searching gaze toward him. "Forgive me, Will, but...for some reason I had the impression you weren't exactly overjoyed to see me the other day."

And he thought he'd been so careful at hiding his reaction. He shifted his weight, not sure how to answer. Any apology would only lead to explanations he was eager to avoid at all costs.

"You took me by surprise, that's all," he finally said.

"A mysterious stranger emerging from your distant past?"

"Something like that. Sixteen seems like a long, long time ago."

She nodded solemnly but said nothing. After an awkward moment, he headed for the door again.

"Anyway, I'm sorry if I seemed less than welcoming." It needed to be said, he decided. Apparently, she was going to be his neighbor and he disliked the idea of this uneasiness around her continuing. That didn't make the words any easier to get out. "You caught me at a bad moment, that's all. But I'm sorry if I gave you the impression I didn't want you here. It was nothing personal."

"I must say, that's a relief to hear."

She smiled, warm and sincere, and for just an instant he was blinded by it, remembering the surge of his blood every time he had been anywhere close to her that last summer.

Before he could make his brain work again, Sage walked up carrying one bulky box.

"What do you have in these, for Pete's sake? Did you pack along every brick from your old place?"

Julia laughed, a light, happy sound that stirred the hair on the back of his neck.

"Not bricks, but close, I'm afraid. Books. I left a lot in storage back in Boise but I couldn't bear to leave them all behind."

So that hadn't changed about her. When she was a kid, she always seemed to have her nose in a book. He and her brother used to tease her unmercifully about being a bookworm.

That last summer, he had been relentless in his efforts

to drag her attention away from whatever book she was reading so she would finally notice him....

He dragged his mind away from the past and the dumb, self-absorbed jerk he'd been. He didn't want to remember those times. What was the damn point? That stupid, eager, infatuated kid was gone, buried under the weight of the years and pain that had piled up since then.

Instead, he left Sage and Julia to talk about books and headed back down the sweeping Brambleberry House stairs. On the way, he passed Anna heading back up, carrying a suitcase in each hand. He tried to take them from her but she shook him off.

"I've got these. There are some bulkier things in the U-Haul you could bring up, though."

"Sure," he answered.

In the entryway on the ground floor, he heard music coming from inside Anna's apartment. Through the open doorway, he caught a glimpse of her television set where a Disney DVD was just starting up.

Julia's twins must have finished playing and come inside. He spotted Julia's boy on the floor in front of the TV, his arm slung across Conan's back. Both of them sensed Will's presence and looked up. He started to greet them but the boy put a finger to his mouth and pointed to Abigail's favorite armchair.

Will followed his gaze and found the girl— Maddie—curled up there, fast asleep.

She looked small and fragile, with her too-pale skin

and thin wrists. There was something going on with her, but he was pretty sure he was better off not knowing.

He waved to the boy, then headed down the porch steps to the waiting U-Haul.

It was nearly empty now except for perhaps a half-dozen more boxes, a finely crafted Mission-style rocking chair and something way in the back, a bulky-looking item wrapped in an old blanket that had been secured with twine.

He went for the rocking chair first. Might as well get the tough stuff out of the way. It was harder to carry than he expected—wide and solid, made of solid oak—but more awkward than really heavy.

He made it without any trouble up the porch steps and was trying to squeeze it through the narrow front door without bunging up the doorframe moldings when Sage came down the stairs.

"Okay, Superman. Let me help you with that."

"I can handle it."

"Only because of your freakish strength, maybe."

He felt his mouth quirk. Sage always managed to remind him he still had the ability to smile.

"I had my can of spinach just an hour ago so I think I've got this covered. There are a few more boxes in the U-Haul. Those ought to keep you busy and out of trouble."

She stuck her tongue out at him and he smiled at the childish gesture, with a sudden, profound gratitude for the friendship of those few people around him who had sustained him through the wrenching pain of the last two years.

"Which is it? Are you Popeye or Superman?"

"Take your pick."

"Or just a stubborn male, like the rest of your gender?" She lifted the front end of the chair. "Even Popeye and Superman need help once in awhile. Besides, we wouldn't want you to throw your back out. Then how would all our work get done around here?"

He knew when he was defeated. With a sigh, he picked up the other end. They had another minor tussle about who should walk backward up the stairs but he won that one simply by turning around and starting up.

She didn't let him gloat for long. "I understand you know our new tenant."

His gaze flashed to hers. *Uh-oh. Here comes the inquisition*, he thought. "Knew. Past tense. A long time ago."

The words were becoming like a mantra since she showed up again in Cannon Beach. *A long time ago.* But not nearly long enough. Like a riptide, the memories just seemed to keep grabbing him out of nowhere and sucking him under.

"She's lovely, isn't she?" Sage pressed as they hit the halfway mark on the stairs. "And those kids of hers are adorable. I can't wait until Eben and Chloe finish up their trip to Europe in a few weeks. Chloe's going to be over the moon at having two new friends."

"How are the wedding plans?" he asked at her mention of her fiancé and his eight-year-old daughter. The question was aimed more at diverting her attention than out of much genuine interest to hear about her upcoming nuptials, but it seemed to work.

Sage made a face. "You know I'm not good at that kind of thing. If I had my way, I would happy with something simple on the beach, just Eben and me and Chloe and the preacher."

"I guess when you marry a gazillionaire hotel magnate, sometimes you have to make sacrifices."

"It's still going to be small, just a few friends at the ceremony than a reception later at the Sea Urchin. I'm leaving all the details to Jade and Stanley Wu."

"Smart woman."

She went on about wedding plans and he listened with half an ear.

In a million years, he never would have expected a hippie-chick like Sage to fall for a California businessman like Eben Spencer but somehow they seemed to fit together.

Sage was more at peace than he'd ever known her, settled in a way he couldn't explain.

She was one of his closest friends and had been since she moved to town five years ago and found herself immediately drawn into Abigail's orbit. He loved her as a little sister and he knew she deserved whatever joy she could find.

He wanted to be happy for her—and most of the time he was—but every once in awhile, seeing the love and happiness that seemed to surround her and Eben when they were together was like a slow, relentless trickle of acid on an open wound.

Despite knowing Julia was inside, he was relieved as hell when they reached the top of the stairs and turned into the apartment.

"Oh, my Stickley! We bought that when I was pregnant with the twins. I know the apartment is furnished but I couldn't bear to leave it behind. Thank you so much for carrying that heavy thing all that way! That goes right here by the window so I can sit in it at night and watch the moonlight shining on the ocean."

He set it down, his mind on the rocking chair he had made Robin when she was pregnant with Cara. It was still sitting in the nursery along with the toddler bed he had made, gathering dust.

He really ought to do something with the furniture. Sage would probably know somebody who could use it....

Not today, he thought abruptly. He wasn't ready for that yet.

He turned on his heel and headed back down the stairs to retrieve that mysterious blanket-wrapped item. When he reached the U-Haul, he stood for a moment studying it, trying to figure out what it might be—and how best to carry it up the Brambleberry House stairs—when the enticing scent of cherry blossoms swirled around him.

"It's a dollhouse." Julia spoke beside him in a low voice and he automatically squared his shoulders, though what he was bracing for, he wasn't quite sure.

"My father made it for me years ago. My…late husband tried to fix it up a little for Maddie but I'm afraid it's still falling apart. I really hope it survived the trip."

So she was a widow. They had that in common, then. He cleared his throat. "Should we take the blanket off?"

She shrugged, which he took for assent. He unwrapped the cord and heard a crunching kind of thud inside. Uh-oh. Not a good sign. With a careful look at her and a growing sense of trepidation, he pulled the blanket away and winced as Julia gasped.

Despite her obvious efforts to protect the dollhouse, the piece hadn't traveled well. The construction looked flimsy to begin with and the roof had collapsed.

One entire support wall had come loose as well and the whole thing looked like it was ready to implode.

"I'm sorry," he said, though the words seemed grossly inadequate.

"It's not your fault. I was afraid it wouldn't survive the trip. Oh, this is going to break Maddie's heart. She loved that little house."

"So did you," he guessed.

She nodded. "For a lot of reasons." She tilted her head, studying the wreckage. "You're the carpentry expert. I don't suppose there's any way I can fix this, is there?"

He gazed down at her, at the fading rays of the sun

that caught gold strands in her hair, at the sorrow marring those lovely features for a lost treasure.

He gave an inward groan. Dammit, he didn't want to do this. But he was such a sucker for a woman in distress. How could he just walk away?

He cleared his throat. "If you want, I could take a look at it. See what I can do."

"Oh, I couldn't ask that of you."

"You didn't ask," he said gruffly.

She sent him a swift look. "No. I didn't."

"I'm kind of slammed with projects right now. It might take me awhile to get to it. And even then, I can't make any guarantees. That's some major damage there. You might be better just starting over."

She forced a smile, though he could see the sadness lingering in her eyes. Her father had made it for her, she had said. He didn't remember much about her father from their summers in Cannon Beach, mostly that the man always seemed impatient and abrupt.

"I can't make any promises," he repeated. "But I'll see what I can do."

"Oh, that would be wonderful. Thank you so much, Will."

Together, they gathered up the shattered pieces of the dollhouse and carried them to his truck, where he set them carefully in the back between his toolbox and ladder.

"I'm happy to pay you for your time and trouble."

As if he would ever accept her money. "Don't worry about it. Let's see if I can fix it first."

She nodded and looked as if she wanted to say something more. To his vast relief, after a moment, she closed her mouth, then returned to the U-Haul for the last few boxes.

Chapter Four

Between the two of them, they were able to carry all but a few of the remaining boxes from the U-Haul up the stairs, where they found Sage and Julia pulling books out of boxes and placing them on shelves.

"You're all so wonderful to help me," Julia said, gratitude coursing through her as she smiled at all three of them. "I have to tell you, I never expected such a warm welcome. I thought it would be weeks before I would even know a soul in Cannon Beach besides Abigail. I haven't even started teaching yet but I feel as if I have instant friends."

Sage smiled. "We're thrilled to have you and the twins here. And I think Abigail would be, too. Don't you think, Will?"

He set down the boxes. "Sure. She always loved kids."

"She was nothing but a big kid herself. Remember how she used to sit out on the porch swing for hours with Cara, swinging and telling stories and singing."

"I remember," he said, his voice rough.

Color flooded Sage's features suddenly. "Oh, Will. I'm sorry."

He shook his head. "Don't, Sage. It's okay. I'd better get the last load of boxes."

He turned and headed down the stairs, leaving behind only the echo of his workboots hitting the wooden steps. Julia turned her confused gaze to Anna and Sage and found them both watching after Will with identical expressions of sadness in their eyes.

"I missed something, obviously," she said softly.

Sage gave Anna a helpless look and the other woman shrugged.

"She'll find out sooner or later," Anna said. "She might as well hear it from us."

"You're right," Sage said. "It just still hurts so much to talk about the whole thing."

"You don't have to tell me anything," Julia said quickly. "I'm sorry if I've wandered into things that are none of my business."

Sage glanced down the stairs as if checking to see if Will was returning. When she was certain he was still outside, she turned back, her voice pitched low. "Will had a daughter. She would have been a couple years younger than your twins. Cara. That's who I was talking about. Abigail adored her. We all did. She was the cutest little thing you've ever seen, just full of energy, with big blue eyes, brown curls and dimples. She was full of sugar, our Cara."

Had a daughter. Not has. An ache blossomed in her chest and she knew she didn't want to hear any more.

But she had learned many lessons over the last few years—one of the earliest was that information was empowering, even if the gaining of it was a process often drenched in pain.

"What happened?" she forced herself to ask.

Sage shook her head, her face inexpressibly sad. Anna squeezed her arm and picked up the rest of the story.

"Cara was killed along with Will's wife, Robin, two years ago." Though Anna spoke in her usual no-nonsense tone, Julia could hear the pain threading through her words.

"They were crossing the street downtown in the middle of the afternoon when they were hit by a drunk tourist in a motorhome," she went on. "Robin died instantly but Cara hung on for two weeks. We all thought—hoped—she was going to pull through but she caught an infection in the hospital in Portland and her little body was too weak and battered to fight it."

She wanted to cry, just sit right there in the middle of the floor and weep for him. More than that, she wanted to race down the stairs and hug her own precious darlings to her.

"Oh, poor Will. He must have been shattered."

"We all were," Sage said. "It was like a light went out of all of us. Will used to be so lighthearted. Like a big tease of an older brother. It's been more than two years since Robin and Cara died and I can count on one hand the number of times I've seen him genuinely smile at something since then."

The ache inside her stretched and tugged and her eyes burned with tears for the teenage boy with the mischievous eyes.

Sage touched her arm. "I'm so glad you're here now."

"Me? Why?"

"Well, you've lost someone, too. You understand, in a way the rest of us can't. I'm sure it would help Will to talk to someone who's experienced some of those same emotions."

Julia barely contained her wince, feeling like the world's biggest fraud.

"Grief is such a solitary, individual thing," she said after an awkward moment. "No one walks the same journey."

Sage smiled and pressed a cheek to Julia's. "I know. But I'm still glad you're here, and I'm sure Will is, too."

Julia was saved from having to come up with an answer to that when she again heard his footsteps on the stairs. A moment later, he came in, muscles bulging beneath the cotton of his shirt as he carried in a trio of boxes.

He had erased any trace of emotion from his features, any sign at all that he contained any emotions at all. Finding out about his wife and daughter explained so much about him. The hardness, the cynicism. The pain in his eyes when he looked at Maddie.

She had a wild urge to take the boxes from him, slip her arms around his waist and hold him until everything was all right again.

"This is the last of it. Where do these go?"

Her words tangled in her throat and she had to clear her throat before she could speak. "The top one belongs in my bedroom. The others are Simon's."

With an abrupt nod, he headed first to her room and then to the one down the hall where Simon slept.

He returned to the living room just as the doorbell downstairs rang through the house.

"Hey, Mom!" Simon yelled up the stairs an instant later. "The pizza guy's here!"

Conan started barking in accompaniment and Julia rolled her eyes at the sudden cacophony of sound. "Are you sure about this? The house was so quiet before we showed up. If you want that quiet again, you'd better speak now while I've still got the U-Haul."

Sage shook her head with a laugh. "No way. I'm not lugging those books back down the stairs. You're stuck here for awhile."

Right now, she couldn't think of anywhere she would rather be. Julia flashed a quick smile to the other two women and Will, grabbed her purse, and headed down the stairs to pay for the pizza.

Simon stood at the door holding on to Conan's collar as the dog wriggled with excitement, his tail wagging a mile a minute.

Her son giggled. "I think he really likes pizza, Mom."

"I guess. Maybe you had better take him into Anna's apartment so he doesn't attack the pizza driver."

With effort, he wrangled the dog through the door and closed the door behind him. Finally, Julia opened the door and found a skinny young man with his cap on backward and his arms full of pizza boxes.

She quickly paid him for the pizza—adding in a hefty tip. She closed the door behind him and backed into the entry, her arms full, and nearly collided with a solid male.

Strong arms came around her to keep her upright.

"Oh," she exclaimed to Will. "I didn't hear you come down the stairs."

"You were talking to the driver," he answered. He quickly released her—much to her regret. She knew she shouldn't have enjoyed that brief moment of contact, but it had been so very long…

She couldn't help noticing the boy she had known now had hard strength in his very grown-up muscles.

"I thought you said the trailer was empty," she said with some confusion as he headed for the door.

"It is. You're done here so I'm heading home."

"You can't leave!" she exclaimed.

He raised an eyebrow. "I can't?"

She held out the boxes in her arms. "You've got to stay for pizza. I ordered way too much for three women and two children."

"Don't forget Conan," he pointed out. "He's crazy about pizza, even though all that cheese is lousy for him."

"Knowing my kids, I'm sure he'll be able to sneak far more than is good for him."

The scent of him reached her, spicy and male and far more enticing than any pizza smells. "I still have too much. Please stay."

He gazed at the door with a look almost of desperation in his eyes. But when he turned back, she thought he might be weakening.

"Please, Will," she pressed.

He opened his mouth to answer but before he could, the door to Abigail's apartment opened and Maddie peeked her head out, looking tousled and sleepy.

"Can we come out now?" she asked.

"As long as the dog's not going to knock me down to get to the Canadian bacon."

At Maddie's giggle, Julia saw a spasm of pain flicker across Will's features and knew the battle was lost.

"I really can't stay." He reached for the doorknob. "Thanks anyway for the invitation, but I've got a lot of work to do at home."

She couldn't push him more, not with that shadow of pain clouding his blue eyes. Surrendering to the inevitable, she simply nodded. "You still need to eat. Take some home with you."

She could see the objections forming on his expression and decided not to take no for an answer. Will Garrett didn't know stubborn until he came up against her.

"What's your pleasure? Pepperoni or Hawaiian? I'd offer you the vegetarian but I think Sage has dibs on that one."

"It's not necessary, really."

"It is to me," she said firmly. "You just spent forty-five minutes helping me haul boxes up. You have to let me repay you somehow. Here, I hope you still like pepperoni and olive."

His eyes widened that she would remember such a detail. She couldn't have explained why—it was just one of those arcane details that stuck in her head. Several times that last summer, they'd gone to Mountain Mike's Pizza in town with her brother and Will always had picked the same thing.

"Maddie, can you hold this for a second?"

She gave the box marked pepperoni to her daughter, then with one hand she opened it and pulled out half the pizza, which she stuck on top of the Hawaiian.

He looked as if he wanted to object, but he said nothing when she handed him the box with the remaining half a pizza in it.

"Here you go. You should have enough for dinner tonight and breakfast in the morning as well. Consider it a tiny way to say thank you for all your hard work."

He shook his head but to her vast relief, he didn't hand the pizza back to her.

"Mom, I can't hold him anymore!" Simon said from behind the door. "He's starving and so am I!"

"You'd better get everyone upstairs for pizza," Will said.

"Right. Good night, then."

She wanted to say more—much more—but with a rambunctious dog and two hungry children clamoring for her attention, she had to be content with that.

Blasted stubborn woman.

Will sat on his deck watching the lights of Cannon Beach flicker on the water as he ate his third piece of pizza.

He had to admit, even lukewarm, it tasted delicious— probably a fair sight better than the peanut butter sandwich he would have scrounged for his meal.

He didn't order pizza very often since half of it usually went to waste before he could get to the leftovers so this was a nice change from TV dinners and fast-food hamburgers.

He really needed to shoot for a healthier diet. Sage was always after him to get more vegetables and fewer preservatives into his diet. He tried but he'd never been a big one for cooking in the first place. He could grill steaks and burgers and the occasional chicken breast but he usually fell short at coming up with something to go alongside the entree.

He fell short in a lot of areas. He sighed, listening to the low rumble of the sea. He spent a lot of his free time puttering around in his dad's shop or sitting out here watching the waves, no matter what the weather. He just hated the emptiness inside the house.

He ought to move, he thought, as he did just about every night at this same time when the silence settled over him with like a scratchy, smothering wool blanket.

He ought to just pick up and make a new start somewhere. Especially now that Julia Hudson Blair had climbed out of the depths of his memories and taken up residence just a few hundred yards away.

She knew.

Sometime during the course of the evening, Sage or Anna must have told her about the accident. He wasn't quite sure how he was so certain, but he had seen a deep compassion in the green of her eyes, a sorrow that hadn't been there earlier.

He washed the pizza down with a swallow of Sam Adams—the one bottle he allowed himself each night.

He knew it shouldn't bother him so much that she knew. Wasn't like it was some big secret. She would find out sooner or later, he supposed.

He just hated that first shock of pity when people first

found out—though he supposed when it came down to it, the familiar sadness from friends like Sage and Anna wasn't much easier.

Somehow seeing that first spurt of pity in Julia's eyes made it all seem more real, more raw.

Her life hadn't been so easy. She was a widow, so she must know a thing or two about loss and loneliness. That didn't make him any more eager to have her around—or her kids.

He shouldn't have made a big deal out of the whole thing. He should have just sucked it up and stayed for pizza with her and Sage and Anna. Instead, his kneejerk reaction had been to flee and he had given into it, something very unlike him.

He sighed and took another swallow of beer. From here, he could see her bedroom light. A dark shape moved across the window and he eased back into the shadows of his empty house.

Why was he making such a big deal about this? Julia meant nothing to him. Less than nothing. He hadn't thought about her in years. Yeah, years ago he had been crazy about her when he was just a stupid, starry-eyed kid. He had dreamed about her all that last summer, when she came back to Cannon Beach without her braces and with curves in all the right places.

First love could be an intensely powerful thing for a sixteen-year-old boy. When she left Cannon Beach, his dreams of a long-distance relationship were quickly dashed when she didn't write to him as she had promised. He had tried to call the phone number she'd given him and left several messages that were never returned.

He was heartbroken for a while but he'd gotten over it. By spring, when he'd taken Robin Cramer to the prom, he had completely forgotten about Julia Hudson and her big green eyes.

Life had taught him that a tiny little nick in his heart left by a heedless fifteen-year-old girl was nothing at all to the pain of having huge, jagged chunks of his soul ripped away.

Now, sixteen years later, Julia was nothing to him. He just needed to shake this weird feeling that the careful order of the life he had painstakingly managed to piece together in the last two years had just been tossed out to sea.

He could think of no earthly reason he shouldn't be able to treat her and her children with politeness, at least.

He couldn't avoid interacting with Julia, for a dozen reasons. Beyond the minor little fact that she lived three houses down, he was still working on renovating several of the Brambleberry House rooms. He couldn't avoid her and he sure as hell couldn't run away like a coward every time he saw her kids.

He looked up at Brambleberry House again and his gaze automatically went to the second-floor window. A shape moved across again and a moment later the light went out and somehow Will felt more alone than ever.

* * *

"Thank you both again for your help today." Julia smiled at Sage and Anna across the table in her new apartment as they finished off the pizza. "I don't know what I would have done without you."

Anna shook her head. "We only helped you with the easy part. Now you have to figure out where to put everything."

"We have dishes in the kitchen and sheets on the beds. Beyond that, everything else can wait until the morning."

"Looks like some of us need to find that path there sooner than others," Sage murmured, gesturing toward Maddie.

"Not me," Maddie instantly protested, but Julia could clearly see she was drooping tonight, with her elbow propped on the table and her head resting on her fist.

Even with her short nap, Maddie still looked tired. Julia sighed. Some days dragged harder than others on Maddie's stamina. They had spent a busy day making all the arrangements to move into Brambleberry House. Maddie had helped carry some of her own things to her bedroom and had delighted in putting her toys and clothes away herself.

With all the craziness of moving in, Julia hadn't been as diligent as usual about making sure Maddie didn't overextend herself and now it looked as if she had reached the limit of her endurance.

"Time for bed, sweetie. Let's get your meds."

"I'm not ready for bed," she protested, sending a pleading look to Anna and Sage, as if they could offer a reprieve. "I want to stay up and help move in."

"I'm tuckered myself," Julia said. "I'll leave all the fun stuff for tomorrow when we're all rested, okay?"

Maddie sighed with a quiet resignation that never failed to break her heart. She caught herself giving into the sorrow and quickly shunted it away. Her daughter was still here. She was a miracle and Julia could never allow herself to forget that.

Before she brought in any other boxes, she had made sure to put Maddie's pill regimen away in a cabinet by the kitchen sink. She poured a glass of water and handed them to her. With the ease of long, grim practice, Maddie downed the half-dozen pills in two swallows, then finished the water to flush down the pills.

Because her daughter seemed particularly tired, Julia helped her into her pajamas then did a quick set of vitals. Everything was within normal ranges for Maddie so Julia pushed away her lingering worry.

"Good night, sweetie," she said after a quick story and kiss. "Your first sleep in the new house!"

"I like this place," Maddie said sleepily as Julia pulled the nightgown over her thin shoulders.

"I like it, too. It feels like home, doesn't it?"

Maddie nodded. "And the lady is nice."

Julia smiled. "Which one? Sage or Anna? I think they're both pretty nice."

Maddie shook her head but her eyes drooped closed before she could answer.

Julia watched her sleep for a moment, marveling again at the lessons in courage and strength and grace her daughter had taught her these last few years.

A miracle, she thought again. As she stood watching over her, she felt the oddest sensation, almost like feather-light fingers touching her cheek.

Weird, she thought. Sage and Anna had warned her Brambleberry House was a typical drafty old house. She would have to do her best to seal up any cracks in Maddie's room.

When she returned to the other room, she found only Simon, curled up in the one corner of the couch not covered in boxes. He had a book in one hand and was petting Conan absently with the other.

What a blessing her son loved to read. Books and his Game Boy had sustained him through many long, boring doctor appointments.

"Did Sage and Anna go downstairs?" she asked.

"I think they're still in the kitchen," Simon answered without looking up from his book.

She heard low, musical laughter before she reached the kitchen. For a moment, she stood in the doorway watching them as they unloaded her grandmother's china into the built-in cabinet.

Here was another blessing. She was overflowing with them. She had come back to Cannon Beach with only a teaching position and her hope that everything would work out. Now she had this great apartment overlooking the sea and, more importantly, two unexpected new friends who were already becoming dear to her.

She didn't think she made a sound but Sage suddenly sensed her presence. She glanced toward her, her exotic tilted eyes lighting in welcome.

"Our girl is all settled for the night?"

Julia nodded. "It was a hectic day. She wore herself out."

"Is she all right?" Anna asked, her features tight with concern.

"Yes. She's fine. She just doesn't have the stamina she used to have." She paused, deciding it was time to reveal everything. "It's one of the long-term side effects of her bone marrow transplant."

"Bone marrow transplant?" Anna exclaimed, her eyes wide with a shock mirrored on Sage's features.

Julia sighed. "Yes. And a round of radiation and two rounds of chemotherapy. I probably should have told you this earlier but Maddie is in remission from acute lymphocytic leukemia."

Chapter Five

Saying the words aloud always left her feeling vaguely queasy, as if she were the one who had endured months of painful treatments, shots, blood draws, the works.

She found it quite a lowering realization that Maddie had faced her cancer ordeal with far more courage than Julia had been able to muster as her mother.

"Oh, Julia." Sage stepped forward and wrapped her into a spontaneous hug. "I'm so sorry you've all had to go through this."

"It's been a pretty bumpy road," she admitted. "But as I said, she's in remission and she's doing well. Much better since the bone marrow transplant. Simon was the donor. We were blessed that they were a perfect match."

"You've had to go through this all on your own?" Anna's dark eyes looked huge and sad.

She knew Anna was referring to Kevin's death and the timing of it. She decided she wasn't quite ready to delve into those explanations just yet so she chose to evade the question.

"I had a strong support network in Boise," she said instead. "Good friends, my brother and his wife, my co-workers at the elementary school there. They all think I'm crazy to move away."

"Why did you?" Anna asked.

"We were all ready for a change. A new start. Three months ago, Maddie's oncologist took a new job at the children's hospital in Portland. Dr. Lee had been such a support and comfort to us and when she moved, it seemed like the perfect time for us to venture back out in the world."

She sometimes felt as if their lives had been on hold for three years. Between Maddie's diagnosis, then Kevin's death, she and her children had endured far too much.

They needed laughter and joy and the peace she had always found by the ocean.

She smiled at the two other women. "I have to tell you both, I was still wondering if I had made a terrible mistake leaving behind our friends and the safe cushion of support we had in Boise, until we saw the for-rent sign out front of Brambleberry House. It seemed like a miracle that we might have the chance to live in the very house I had always loved so much when I was a little girl, the house where I had always found peace. I took that sign as an omen that everything would be okay."

"We're so glad you found us," Anna said.

"You belong here," Sage added. She squeezed Julia's fingers with one hand and reached for Anna's hand with the other, linking them all together and Julia had to fight back tears, overwhelmed by their easy acceptance of her.

She realized she felt happier standing in this warm kitchen with these women than she could remember being in a long, long time.

"Thank you," she said softly. "Thank you both."

"You smell that?" Sage demanded after a moment.

Anna rolled her eyes. "Cut it out, Sage."

"Smell what?" Julia asked.

"Freesia," Sage answered. "You smelled it, too, didn't you?"

"I thought it was coming from the open window."

Sage shook her head. "Nope. As much as she loved it, Abigail could never get any freesia bulbs to survive in her garden. Our microclimate is just not conducive to them."

"I hope you're not squeamish about ghosts," Anna said after a long sigh. "Sage insists Abigail is still here at Brambleberry House, that she flits through the house leaving behind the freesia perfume she always wore."

Julia blinked, astonished. It seemed preposterous— until she remembered Maddie's words that the lady was nice, and that soft brush against her skin when she had been standing in Maddie's room looking over her daughter almost as if someone had touched her tenderly.

She fought back a shiver.

"You don't buy it?" she said to Anna.

Anna laughed. "I don't know. I usually tend to fall on the side of logic and reason. My intellect tells me it's a complete impossibility. But then, I can't put anything past Abigail. It wouldn't surprise me at all if she decided to defy the rules of metaphysics and stick around in this house she loved. If it's at all within the realm of possibility, Abigail would find a way."

"And Conan is her familiar," Sage added. "You probably ought to know that up front, too. I think the two of them are a team. If Abigail is the brains of the outfit, he's the muscle."

"Okay, now you're obviously putting me on."

Sage shook her head.

"Conan. The dog."

Sage grinned. "Don't look at me like I'm crazy. Just watch and see. The dog is spooky."

"On that, at least, we can agree," Anna said, setting the last majolica teacup in the cupboard. "He's far smarter than your average dog."

"I've seen that much already," Julia admitted. "I'm sorry, but it's a bit of a stretch for me to go from thinking he's an uncommonly smart dog to buying the theory that he's some kind of conduit from the netherworld."

Sage laughed. "Put like that, it does sound rather ridiculous, doesn't it? Just keep your eyes open. You can judge for yourself after you've been here awhile. I wanted to put a disclosure in the rental agreement about Abigail but Anna wouldn't let me."

Anna made a face. "It's a little tough to find an attorney who will add a clause that we might have a ghost in the house."

"There's no *might* about it. You wait and see, Julia."

A ghost and a dog/medium. She supposed there were worst things she could be dealing with in an apartment. "I hope she is still here. I can't imagine Abigail would be anything but a benevolent spirit."

Sage grinned at her. Anna shook her head, but she was smiling as well. "I see I'm outnumbered in the sanity department."

"You're just better at being a grown-up," Sage answered. Her teasing slid away quickly, though, replaced with concern. "And on that note, is there anything special we need to worry about with Maddie? Environmental things she shouldn't be exposed to or anything?"

Julia sighed. She would much rather ponder lighthearted theories of the supernatural than bump up against the harsh reality of her daughter's illness and recovery.

"It's a tough line I walk between wrapping her up in cotton wool to protect her and encouraging as normal a life as possible. Most of the time she's fine, if a little more subdued than she once was. You probably wouldn't know it but she used to be the spitfire of the twins. When they were toddlers, she was always the one leading Simon into trouble."

She gave a wobbly smile and was warmed when Anna reached out and squeezed her hand.

A moment passed before she could trust her voice to continue. "Right now we need to work on trying to regain the strength she lost through the month she spent in the hospital with the bone marrow transplant. I hope by Christmas things will be better."

Sage smiled. "Well, now you've got two more of us—four, counting Abigail and Conan—on your side."

"Thank you," she whispered, immeasurably touched at their effortless acceptance of her and her children.

After Simon was finally settled in bed, Julia stood in her darkened bedroom gazing out at the ripples of the sea gleaming in the moonlight. Though she had a million things to do—finding bowls they could use for cereal in the morning hovered near the top of her list—she decided she needed this moment to herself to think, without rushing to take care of detail after detail.

Offshore some distance, she could see the moving lights of a sea vessel cutting through the night. She watched it for a moment, then her gaze inexorably shifted to the houses along the shore.

There was the cottage where her family had always

stayed, sitting silent and dark. Beyond that was Will Garrett's house. A light burned inside a square cedar building set away from the house. His father's workshop, she remembered. Now it would be Will's.

She glanced at her watch and saw it was nearly midnight. What was he working on so late? And did he spend his time out in his workshop to avoid the emptiness inside his house?

She pressed a hand to her chest at the ache there. How did he bear the pain of losing his wife and his child? She remembered the vast sorrow in his gaze when he had looked at Maddie and she wanted so much to be able to offer some kind of comfort to him.

She sensed he wouldn't want her to try. Despite his friendship with Sage and Anna, Will seemed to hold himself apart, as if he had used his carpentry skills to carefully hammer out a wall between himself and the rest of the world.

She ached for him, but she knew there was likely very little she could do to breach those walls.

She could try.

The thought whispered through her head with soft subtlety. She shook her head at her own subconscious. No. She had enough on her plate right now, moving to a new place, taking on a new job, dealing with twins on her own, one of whom still struggled with illness.

She didn't have the emotional reserves to take on anyone else's pain. She knew it, but as the peace of the house settled around her, she had the quiet conviction that she could at least offer him her friendship.

As if in confirmation, the sweet, summery scent of freesia drifted through the room. She smiled.

"Abigail, if you are still here," she whispered, "thank you. For this place, for Anna and Sage. For everything."

For just an instant, she thought she felt again the gentle brush of fingers against her cheek.

Will managed to avoid his new neighbors for several days, mostly because he was swamped with work. He was contracted to do the carpentry work on a rehab project in Manzanita. The job was behind schedule because of other subcontractors' delays and the developer wanted the carpentry work done yesterday.

Will was pouring every waking moment into it, leaving his house before the sun was up and returning close to midnight every night.

He didn't mind working hard. Having too much work to do was a damn sight better than having too little. Building something with his hands helped fill the yawning chasm of his life.

But his luck where his neighbors were concerned ran out a week after he had helped carry boxes up to the second-floor apartment of Brambleberry House.

By Friday, most of the basic work on the construction job was done and the only thing left was for him to install the custom floor and ceiling moldings the developer had ordered from a mill in Washington State. They hadn't been delivered yet and until they arrived, he had nothing to do.

Finally he returned to Cannon Beach, to his empty house and his empty life.

After showering off the sawdust and sweat from a hard day's work, he was grilling a steak on the deck—his nightly beer in hand—watching tourists fly kites and play in the sand in the pleasant early evening breeze when he suddenly heard excited barking.

A moment later, a big red mutt bounded into view, trailing the handle of his retractable leash.

As soon as he spied Will, he switched directions and bounded up the deck steps, his tongue lolling as he panted heavily.

"You look like a dog on the lam."

Conan did that weird grin thing of his and Will glanced down the beach to see who might have been on the other end of the leash. He couldn't see anyone—not really surprising. Though he seemed pondeorus most of the time, Conan could pour on the juice when he wanted to escape his dreaded leash and be several hundred yards down the beach before you could blink.

When he turned back to the dog, he found him sniffing with enthusiasm around the barbecue.

"No way," Will muttered. "Get your own steak. I'm not sharing."

Conan whined and plopped down at his feet with

such an obviously feigned morose expression that Will had to smile. "You're quite the actor, aren't you? No steak for you tonight but I will get you a drink. You look like you could use it."

He found the bowl he usually used for Conan and filled it from the sink. When he walked back through the sliding doors, he heard a chorus of voices calling the dog's name.

Somehow, he supposed he wasn't really surprised a moment later when Julia Blair and her twins came into view from the direction of Brambleberry House.

Conan barked a greeting, his head hanging over the deck railing. Three heads swiveled in their direction and even from here, he could see the relief in Julia's green eyes when she spotted the dog.

"There you are, you rascal," she exclaimed.

With her hair held back from her face in a ponytail, she looked young and lovely in the slanted early evening light. Though he knew it was unwise, part of him wanted to just sit and savor the sight of her, a little guilty reward for putting in a hard day's work.

Shocked at the impulse, he set down Conan's bowl so hard some water slopped over the side.

"I'm so sorry," Julia called up. Though he wanted to keep them off the steps like he was some kind of medieval knight defending his castle from assault, he stood mutely by as she and her twins walked up the stairs to the deck.

"We were taking him for a walk on the beach," Julia went on, "but we apparently weren't moving quickly enough for him."

"It's my fault," the boy—Simon—said, his voice morose. "Mom said I had to hold his leash tight and I tried, I really did, but I guess I wasn't strong enough."

"I'm sure it's not your fault," Will said through a throat that suddenly felt tight. "Conan can be pretty determined when he sets his mind to something."

Simon grinned at him with a new warmth. "I guess he had his mind set on running away."

"We were going to get an ice cream," the girl said in her whispery voice. He had no choice but to look at her, with her dark curls and blue eyes. A sense of frailty clung to her, as if the slightest breeze would pick her up and carry her out to sea.

He didn't know how to talk to her—didn't know if he could. But he had made a pledge not to hurt others simply because he was in pain. He supposed that included little dark-haired sea sprites.

"That sounds like fun. A great thing to do on a pretty summer night like tonight."

"My favorite ice cream is strawberry cheesecake," she announced. "I really hope they have some."

"Not me," Simon announced. "I like bubblegum. Especially when it's blue bubblegum."

To his dismay, Julia's daughter crossed the deck until she was only a few feet away. She looked up at him out of serious eyes. "What about you, Mr. Garrett?" Maddie asked. "Do you like ice cream?"

Surface similarities aside, she was not at all like his roly-poly little Cara, he reminded himself. "Sure. Who doesn't?"

"What kind is your favorite?"

"Hmmm. Good question. I hate to be boring but I really like plain old vanilla."

Simon hooted. "That's what my mom's favorite flavor is, too. With all the good flavors out there— licorice or coconut or chocolate chunk—why would you ever want plain vanilla? That's just weird."

"Simon!" Julia's cheeks flushed and he thought again how extraordinarily lovely she was—not much different from the girl he'd been so crazy about nearly two decades ago.

"Well, it is," Simon insisted.

"You don't tell someone they're weird," Julia said.

"I didn't say *he* was weird. Just that eating only vanilla ice cream is weird."

Will found himself fighting a smile, which startled him all over again. "Okay, I'll admit I also like praline ice cream and sometimes even chocolate chip on occasion. Is that better?"

Simon snickered. "I guess so."

He felt the slightest brush of air and realized it was Maddie touching his arm with her small, pale hand. Suddenly he couldn't seem to catch his breath, aching inside.

"Would you like to come with us to get an ice-cream cone, Mr. Garrett?" she asked in her breathy voice. "I bet if you were holding Conan's leash, he couldn't get away."

He glanced at her sweet little features then at Julia. The color had climbed even higher on her cheekbones and she gave him an apologetic look before turning back to her daughter.

"Honey, I'm sure Mr. Garrett is busy. It smells like he's cooking a steak for his dinner."

"Which I'd better check on. Hang on."

He lifted the grill and found his porterhouse a little on the well-done side, but still edible. He shut off the flame, using the time to consider how to answer the girl.

He shouldn't be so tempted to go with them. It was an impulse that shocked the hell out of him.

He had spent two years avoiding social situations except with his close friends. But suddenly the idea of sitting here alone eating his dinner and watching others enjoy life seemed unbearable.

How could he possibly go with them, though? He wasn't sure he trusted himself to be decent for an hour or so, the time it would take to walk to the ice-cream place, enjoy their cones, then walk home.

What if something set him off and brought back that bleak darkness that always seemed to hover around the edges of his psyche? The last thing he wanted to do was hurt these innocent kids.

"Thanks for the invitation," he said, "but I'd better stay here and finish my dinner."

Conan whined and butted his head against Will's leg, almost as if urging Will to reconsider.

"We can wait for you to eat," Simon said promptly. "We don't mind, do we, Mom?"

"Simon, Mr. Garrett is busy. We don't want to badger him." She met his gaze, her green eyes soft with an expression he couldn't identify. "Though we would love to have you come along. All of us."

"I don't want you to have to wait for me to eat when you've got strawberry cheesecake and bubblegum ice-cream cones calling your name."

Julia nodded rather sadly, as if she had expected his answer. "Come on, kids. We'd better be on our way."

Conan whined again. Will gazed from the dog to Julia and her family, then he shook his head. "Then again, I guess there's no reason I can't warm my steak up again when we get back from the ice-cream parlor. I'm not that hungry right now anyway."

His statement was met with a variety of reactions. Conan barked sharply, Julia's eyes opened wide with surprise, Simon gave a happy shout and Maddie clapped her hands with delight.

It had been a long time since anyone had seemed so thrilled about his company, he thought as he carried his steak inside to cover it with foil and slide it in the refrigerator.

He didn't know what impulse had prompted him to agree to go along with them. He only knew it had been a long while since he had allowed himself to enjoy the quiet peace of an August evening on the shore.

Maybe it was time.

Chapter Six

This was a mistake of epic proportions.

Will walked alongside Julia while her twins moved ahead with Conan. Simon raced along with the dog, holding tightly to his leash as the two of them scared up a shorebird here and there and danced just out of reach of the waves. Maddie seemed content to walk sedately toward the ice-cream stand in town, stopping only now and again to pick something up from the sand, study it with a serious look, then plop it in her pocket.

Will was painfully conscious of the woman beside him. Her hair shimmered in the dying sunlight, her cheeks were pinkened from the wind, and the soft, alluring scent of cherry blossoms clung to her, feminine and sweet.

He couldn't come up with a damn thing to say and he felt like he was an awkward sixteen-year-old again.

Accompanying her little family to town was just about the craziest idea he had come up with in a long, long time.

She didn't seem to mind the silence but he finally decided good manners compelled him to at least make a stab at conversation.

"How are you settling in?" he asked.

She smiled softly. "It's been lovely. Perfect. You know, I wasn't sure I was making the right choice to move here but everything has turned out far better than I ever dreamed."

"The apartment working out for you, then?"

"It's wonderful. We love it at Brambleberry House. Anna and Sage have become good friends and the children love being so close to the ocean. It's been a wonderful adventure for us all so far."

He envied her that, he realized. The sense of adventure, the willingness to charge headlong into the unknown. He had always been content to stay in the house where he had been raised. He loved living on the coast—waking up to the sound of scoters and grebes, sleeping to the murmuring song of the sea—but lately he sometimes felt as if he were suffocating here. It was impossible to miss the way everyone in town guarded their words around him and worse, watched him out of sad, careful eyes.

Maybe it was time to move on. It wasn't a new

thought but as he walked beside Julia toward the lights of town, he thought perhaps he ought to do just as she had—start over somewhere new.

She was looking at him in expectation, as if she had said something and was waiting for him to respond. He couldn't think what he might have missed and he hesitated to ask her to repeat herself. Instead, he decided to pick a relatively safe topic.

"School starts in a few weeks, right?" he asked.

"A week from Tuesday," she said after a small pause. "I plan to go in and start setting up my classroom tomorrow."

"Does it take you a whole week to set up?"

"Oh, at least a week!" Animation brightened her features even more. "I'm way behind. I've got bulletin boards to decorate, class curriculum to plan, students' pictures and names to memorize. Everything."

Her voice vibrated with excitement and despite his discomfort, he almost smiled. "You can't wait, can you?"

She flashed him a quick look. "Is it that obvious?"

"I'm glad you've found something you enjoy. I'll admit, back in the day, I wouldn't have pegged you for a schoolteacher."

She laughed. "I guess my plans to be a rich and famous diva some day kind of fell by the wayside. Teaching thirty active fifth-graders isn't quite as exciting as going on tour and recording a platinum-selling record."

"I bet you're good at it, though."

She blinked in surprise, then gave him a smile of such pure, genuine pleasure that he felt his chest tighten.

"Thank you, Will. That means a lot to me."

Their gazes met and though it had been a long, long time, he knew he didn't mistake the currents zinging between them.

A gargantuan mistake.

He was almost relieved when they caught up with Maddie, who had slowed her steps considerably.

"You doing okay, cupcake?" Julia asked.

"I'm fine, Mommy," she assured her, though her features were pale and her mouth hung down a little at the edges.

He wondered again what the story was here—why Julia watched her so carefully, why Maddie seemed so frail—but now didn't seem the appropriate time to ask.

"Do you need a piggyback ride the rest of the way to the ice-cream stand?" Julia asked.

Maddie shook her head with more firmness than before, as if that brief rest had been enough for her. "I can make it, I promise. We're almost there, aren't we?"

"Yep. See, there's the sign with the ice-cream cone on it."

Somehow Maddie slipped between them and folded her hand in her mother's. She smiled up at Will and his chest ached all over again.

"I love this place," Maddie announced when they drew closer to Murphy's Ice Cream.

"I do, too," Will told her. "I've been coming here for ice cream my whole life."

She looked intrigued. "Really? My mom said she used to come here, too, when she was little." She paused to take a breath before continuing. "Did you ever see her here?"

He glanced at Julia and saw her cheeks had turned pink and he wondered if she was remembering holding hands under one of the picnic tables that overlooked the beach and stealing kisses whenever her brother wasn't looking.

"I did," he said gruffly, wishing those particular memories had stayed buried.

Maddie looked as if she wanted to pursue the matter but by now they had reached Murphy's.

He hadn't thought this whole thing through, he realized as they approached the walk-up window. Rats. Inside, he could see Lacy Murphy Walker, who went to high school with him and whose family had owned and operated the ice-cream parlor forever.

She had been one of Robin's best friends—and as much as he loved her, he was grimly aware that Lacy also happened to be one of the biggest gossips in town.

"Hi, Will." She beamed with some surprise. "Haven't seen you in here in an age."

He had no idea how to answer that so he opted to stick with a polite smile.

"We're sure loving the new cabinets in the back," she went on. "You did a heck of a job on them. I was saying the other day how much more storage space we have now."

"Thanks, Lace."

Inside, he could see the usual assortment of tourists but more than a few local faces he recognized. The scene was much the same on the picnic tables outside.

His neck suddenly itched from the speculative glances he was getting from those within sight—and especially from Lacy.

She hadn't stopped staring at him and at Julia and her twins since he walked up to the counter.

"You folks ready to order?"

He hadn't been lumped into a *folks* in a long time and it took him a moment to adjust.

Sometimes he thought that was one of the things he had missed the most the last two years, being part of a unit, something bigger and better than himself.

"Hang on," he said, turning back to Julia and her twins. "Have you decided?" he asked, in a voice more terse than he intended.

"Bubblegum!" Simon exclaimed. "In a sugar cone."

Lacy wrote it down with a smile. "And for the young lady?"

Maddie gifted Lacy with a particularly sweet smile. "Strawberry cheesecake, please," she whispered. "I would like a sugar cone, too."

"Got it." Again Lacy turned her speculative gaze at him and Julia, standing together at the counter. "And for the two of you?"

The two of you. He wanted to tell her there was no

two of you. They absolutely were *not* a couple, just two completely separate individuals who happened to walk down the beach together for ice cream.

"Two scoops of vanilla in a sugar cone," he said.

"Make that two of those." Julia smiled at Lacy and he felt a little light-headed. It was only because he hadn't eaten, he told himself. Surely his reaction had nothing to do with the cherry blossom scent of her that smelled sweeter than anything coming out of the ice cream shop.

Lacy gave them the total and Will pulled out his wallet.

"My treat," he said, sliding a bill to Lacy.

She reached for it at the same time Julia did.

"It is not!" Julia exclaimed. "You weren't even planning to come along until we hounded you into it. Forget it, I'm paying."

Even more speculative glances were shooting their way. He could see a couple of his mother's friends inside and was afraid they would be on the phone to her at her retirement village in San Diego before Lacy even scooped their cones.

Above all, he wanted to avoid attention and just win this battle so they could find a place to sit, preferably one out of view of everyone inside.

"Nobody hounded anybody. I wanted to come." *For one brief second of insanity,* he thought, but didn't add. "I'm paying this time. You can pick it up next time."

The minute the words escaped his mouth, he saw Lacy's eyes widen. *Next time,* he had said. Rats. He could just picture the conversation that would be buzzing around town within minutes.

You hear about Will Garrett? He's finally dating again, the new teacher living in Abigail's house. The pretty widow with those twins. Remember, her family used to rent the old Turner place every summer.

He grimaced to himself, knowing there wasn't a darn thing he could do about it. When a person lived in the same town his whole life, everybody seemed to think they had a stake in his business.

"Are you sure?" Julia still looked obstinate.

He nodded. "Take it, Lacey," he said.

To his vast relief, she ended the matter by stuffing the bill into the cash register and handing him his change.

"It should just be a minute," she said in a chirpy kind of voice. She disappeared from the counter, probably to go looking for her cell phone so she could start spreading the word.

"Thank you," Julia said, though she still looked uncomfortable about letting him treat.

"No problem."

"It really doesn't seem fair. You didn't even want to come with us."

"I'm here, aren't I? It's fine."

She looked as if she had something more to say but after a moment she closed her mouth and let the matter rest when Lacy returned with the twins' cones.

"Here you go. The other two are coming right up."

"Great service as always, Lacy," he said when she handed him and Julia their cones. "Thanks."

"Oh, no problem, Will." She smiled brightly. "And let me just say for the record that it's so great to see you out enjoying…ice cream again."

Heat soaked his face and he could only hope he wasn't blushing. He hadn't blushed in about two decades and he sure as hell didn't want to start now.

"Right," he mumbled, and was relieved when Simon spoke up.

"Hey, Mom, our favorite table is empty. Can we sit out there and watch for whales?"

Julia smiled and shook her head ruefully. "We've been here twice and sat at the same picnic table both times. I guess that makes it our favorite."

She studied Will. "Are you in a hurry to get back or do you mind eating our cones here?"

He would rather just take a dip in the cold waters of the Pacific right about now, if only to avoid the watching eyes of everyone in town. Instead, he forced a smile.

"No big rush. Let's sit down."

He made the mistake of glancing inside the ice-cream parlor one time as he was sliding into the picnic table across from her—just long enough to see several heads swivel quickly away from him.

With a sigh, he resigned himself to the rumors. Nothing he could do about them now anyway.

* * *

She was quite certain Conan was a canine but just now he was looking remarkably like the proverbial cat with its mouth stuffed full of canary feathers.

Julia frowned at the dog, who settled beside the picnic table with what looked suspiciously like a grin. Sage and Anna said he had an uncanny intelligence and some hidden agenda but she still wasn't sure she completely bought it.

More likely, he was simply anticipating a furtive taste of one of the twins' cones.

If Conan practically hummed with satisfaction, Will resembled the plucked canary. He ate his cone with a stoicism that made it obvious he wasn't enjoying the treat—or the company—in the slightest.

She might have been hurt if she didn't find it so terribly sad.

She grieved for him, for the boy she had known with the teasing smile and the big, generous heart. His loss was staggering, as huge as the Pacific, and she wanted so desperately to ease it for him.

What power did she have, though? Precious little, especially when he would only talk in surface generalities about mundane topics like the tide schedule and the weather.

She tried to probe about the project he was working on, an intriguing rehabilitation effort down the coast, but he seemed to turn every question back to her and she was tired of talking about herself.

She was also tired of the curious eyes inside. Good heavens, couldn't the poor man go out for ice cream without inciting a tsunami of attention? If he wasn't being so unapproachable, she would have loved to give their tongues something to wag about.

How would Will react if she just grabbed the cone out of his hand, tossed it over her shoulder into the sand, and planted a big smacking kiss on his mouth, just for the sheer wicked thrill of watching how aghast their audience might turn?

It was an impulse from her youth, when she had been full of silly dreams and impetuous behavior. She wouldn't do it now, of course. Not only would a kiss horrify Will but her children were sitting at the table and they wouldn't understand the subtleties of social tit-for-tat.

The idea was tempting, though. And not just to give the gossips something to talk about.

She sighed. It would be best all the way around if she just put those kind of thoughts right out of her head. She had been alone for two years and though she might have longed for a man's touch, she wasn't about to jump into anything with someone still deep in the grieving process.

"What project are you working on next at Bramble-berry House?" she asked him.

"New ceiling and floor moldings in Abigail's old apartment, where Anna lives now," he answered. "On the project I'm working on in Manzanita, the developer ordered some custom patterns. I liked them and showed them to Anna and she thought they would be perfect for Brambleberry House so we ordered extra."

"What was wrong with the old ones?"

"They were cracking and warped in places from water damage a long time ago. We tried to repair them but it was becoming an endless process. And then when she decided to take down a few walls, the moldings in the different rooms didn't match so we decided to replace them all with something histori-cally accurate."

He started to add more, but Maddie slid over to him and held out her cone.

"Mr. Garrett, would you like to try some of my straw-berry cheesecake ice cream? It's really good."

A slight edge of panic appeared around the edges of his gaze. "Uh, no thanks. Think I'll stick with my vanilla."

She accepted his answer with equanimity. "You might change your mind, though," she said, with her in-nate generosity. "How about if I eat it super slow? That way if decide you want some after all, I'll still have some left for you to try later, okay?"

He blinked and she saw the nerves give way to as-tonishment. "Uh, thanks," he said, looking so touched at the small gesture that her heart broke for him all over again.

Maddie smiled her most endearing smile, the particu-larly charming one she had perfected on doctors over the years. "You're welcome. Just let me know if you want a taste. I don't mind sharing, I promise."

He looked like a man who had just been stabbed in the heart and Julia suddenly couldn't bear his pain. In desperation, she sought a way to distract him.

"What will you do on Brambleberry House after you finish the moldings?" she finally asked.

He looked grateful for the diversion. "Uh, your apartment is mostly done but the third-floor rooms still need some work. Little stuff, mostly, but inconvenient to try to live around. I figured I would wait to start until after Sage is married and living part-time in the Bay Area with Eben and Chloe."

"I understand they're coming back soon from an extended trip overseas. We've heard a great deal about them from Sage and Anna. The twins can't wait to meet Chloe."

"She's a good kid. And Eben is good for Sage. That's the important thing."

He was a man who loved his friends, she realized. That, at least, hadn't changed over the years.

He seemed embarrassed by his statement and quickly returned to talking about the repairs planned for Brambleberry House. She listened to his deep voice as she savored the last of her cone, thinking it was a perfect summer evening.

The children finished their treats—Maddie's promise to Will notwithstanding—and were romping with

Conan in the sand. Their laugher drifted on the breeze above the sound of the ocean.

For just an instant, she was transported back in time, sitting with Will atop a splintery picnic table, eating ice-cream cones and laughing at nothing and talking about their dreams.

By unspoken agreement, they stood, cones finished, and started walking back down the beach while Conan herded the twins along ahead of them.

"I'm boring you to tears," Will said after some time. "I'm sorry. I, uh, don't usually go on and on like that about my work."

She shook her head. "You're not boring me. On the contrary. I enjoy hearing about what you do. You love it, don't you?"

"It's just a job. Not something vitally important to the future of the world like educating young minds."

She made a face. "My, you have a rosy view of educators, don't you?"

"I always had good teachers when I was going to school."

"Good teachers wouldn't have anywhere to teach those young minds if not for great carpenters like you," she pointed out. "The work you've done on Brambleberry House is lovely. The kitchen cupboards are as smooth as a satin dress. Anna told me you made them all by hand."

"It's a great old house. I'm trying my best to do it justice."

They walked in silence for a time and Julia couldn't escape the grim realization that she was every bit as attracted to him now as she had been all those years ago.

Not true, she admitted ruefully. Technically, anyway. She was far *more* aware of him now, as a full-grown woman—with a woman's knowledge and a woman's needs—than she ever would have been as a naive, idealistic fifteen-year-old girl.

He was bigger than he had been then, several inches taller and much more muscled. His hair was cut slightly shorter than it had been when he was a teenager and he had a few laugh lines around his mouth and his eyes, though she had a feeling those had been etched some time ago.

She was particularly aware of his hands, square-tipped and strong, with the inevitable battle scars of a man who used them in creative and constructive ways.

She didn't want to notice anything about him and she certainly wasn't at all thrilled to find herself attracted to him again. She couldn't afford it. Not when she and her children were just finding their way again.

Hadn't she suffered enough from emotionally unavailable men?

"Look what I found, Mom!" Maddie uncurled her fingers to reveal a small gnarled object. "What is it?"

As she studied the object, Julia held her daughter's hand, trying not to notice how thin her fingers seemed.

It appeared to be an agate but was an odd color, greenish gray with red streaks in it.

"We forgot to bring our rocky coast field book, didn't we? We'll have to look it up when we get back to the house."

"Do you know, Mr. Garrett?" Maddie presented the object for Will's inspection.

"I'm afraid I'm not much of a naturalist," he said, rather curtly. "Sage is your expert in that department. She can tell you in a second."

"Oh. Okay." Maddie's shoulders slumped, more from fatigue than disappointment, Julia thought, but Will didn't pick up on it. Guilt flickered in his expression.

"I can look at it," he said after a moment. "Let's see."

Will reached for her hand and he examined the contents carefully. "Wow. This is quite a find. It's a bloodstone agate."

"I want to see," Simon said.

"It's pretty rare," Will said. He talked to them about some of the other treasures they could find beachcombing on the coast until they reached his house.

"I guess this is your stop," Julia said as they stood at the steps of his deck.

He glanced up the steps, as if eager to escape, then looked back at them. "I'll walk you the rest of the way to Brambleberry House. It's nearly dark. I wouldn't want you walking on your own."

It was only three houses, she almost said, but he

looked so determined to stick it out that she couldn't bring herself to argue.

"Thank you," she said, then gave Maddie a careful look. Her daughter hadn't said much for some time, since finding the bloodstone.

"Is it piggyback time?" Julia asked quietly.

Maddie shrugged, her features dispirited. "I guess so. I really wanted to make it the whole way on my own this time."

"You made it farther this time than last time. And farther still than the time before. Come on, pumpkin. Your chariot awaits." Julia crouched down and her daughter climbed aboard.

"I can carry her," Will said, though he looked as if he would rather stick a nail gun to his hand and pull the switch.

"I've got her," she answered, aching for him all over again. "But you can make sure Simon and Conan stay away from the surf."

They crossed the last hundred yards to Brambleberry House in silence. When they reached the back gate, Will held it open for them and they walked inside where the smells of Abigail's lush late-summer flowers surrounded them in warm welcome.

She eased Maddie off her back. "You two take Conan inside to get a drink from Anna while I talk to Mr. Garrett, okay?"

"Okay," Simon said, and headed up the steps. Maddie

followed more slowly but a moment later Julia and Will were alone with only the sound of the wind sighing in the tops of the pine trees.

"What's wrong with Maddie?"

His quiet voice cut through the peace of the night and she instinctively bristled, wanting to protest that nothing was wrong with her child. Absolutely nothing. Maddie was perfect in every way.

The words tangled in her throat. "She's recovering from a bone marrow transplant," she answered in a low voice to match his. It wasn't any grand secret and he certainly deserved to know, though she didn't want to go through more explanations.

"It's been four months but she hasn't quite regained her strength. She's been a fighter through everything life has thrown at her the last two and a half years, though—two rounds of chemo and a round of radiation—so I know it's only a matter of time before she'll be back to her old self."

Chapter Seven

He heard her words as if she whispered them on the wind from a long distance away.

Bone marrow transplant. Chemotherapy. Radiation. Cancer.

He had suspected Maddie was ill, but *cancer*. Damn it. The thought of that sweet-faced little girl enduring that kind of nightmare plowed into him like a semitruck and completely knocked him off his pins.

"I'm sorry, Julia."

The words seemed horrifyingly inadequate but he didn't have the first idea what else to say in this kind of situation. Besides, hadn't he learned after the dark abyss of the last two years that sometimes the simplest of sentiments meant the most?

The sun had finally slipped beyond the horizon and in the dusky twilight, she looked young and lovely and as fragile as her daughter.

"It's been a long, tough journey," she answered. "But I have great hope that we're finally starting to climb through to the other side."

He envied her that hope, he realized. That's what had been missing in his world for two years—for too long there had seemed no escape to the unrelenting pain. He missed Robin, he missed Cara, he missed the man he used to be.

But this wasn't about him, he reminded himself. One other lesson he had learned since the accident that stole his family was that very few people made it through life unscathed, without suffering or pain, and Julia had obviously seen more than her share.

"A year and a half, you said. So you must have had to cope with losing your husband in the midst of dealing with Maddie's cancer?"

In the twilight, he saw her mouth open then close, as if she wanted to say something but changed her mind.

"Yes," she finally answered, though he had a feeling that wasn't what she intended to tell him. "I guess you can see why I felt like we needed a fresh start."

"She's okay now, you said?"

"She's been in remission for a year. The bone

marrow transplant was more a precaution because the second round of chemo destroyed her immune system. We were blessed that Simon could be the donor. But as you can imagine, we're all pretty sick of hospitals and doctors by now."

He released a breath, his mind tangled in the vicious thorns of remembering those last terrible two weeks when Cara had clung to life, when he had cried and prayed and begged for another chance for his broken and battered little girl.

For nothing.

His prayers hadn't done a damn bit of good.

"It's kind of surreal, isn't it?" Julia said after a moment. "Who would have thought all those summers ago when we were young that one day we'd be standing here in Abigail's garden together talking about my daughter's cancer treatment?"

He had a sudden, savage need to pummel something—to yank the autumn roses up by the roots, to shatter the porch swing into a million pieces, to hack the limbs off Abigail's dogwood bushes.

"Life is the cruelest bitch around," he said, and the bitter words seemed to scrape his throat bloody and raw. "Makes you wonder what the hell the point is."

She lifted shocked eyes to his. "Oh, Will. I'm so sorry," she whispered, and before he realized her intentions, she reached out and touched his arm in sympathy.

For just a moment the hair on his arm lifted and he

forgot his bitterness, held captive by the gentle brush of skin against skin. He ached for the tenderness of a woman's touch—no, of *Julia's* touch— at the same time it terrified him.

He forced himself to take a step back. Cool night air swirled between them and he wondered how it was possible for the temperature to dip twenty degrees in a millisecond.

"I'd better go." His voice still sounded hoarse. "Your kids probably need you inside."

Her color seemed higher than it had been earlier and he thought she looked slightly disconcerted. "I'm sure you're right. Good night, then. And…thank you for the ice cream and the company. I enjoyed both."

She paused for the barest of moments, as if waiting for him to respond. When the silence dragged on, an instant's disappointment flickered in her eyes and she began to climb the porch steps.

"You're welcome," he said when she reached the top step. She turned with surprise.

"And for the record," he went on, "I haven't enjoyed much of anything for a long time but tonight was… nice."

Her brilliant smile followed him as let himself out the front gate and headed down the dark street toward his home, a journey he had made a thousand times.

He didn't need to think about where he was going, which left his mind free to wander through dark alleys.

Cancer. That cute little girl. Hell.

Poor thing. Julia said it was in remission, that things were better except lingering fatigue. Still, he knew this was just one more reason he needed to maintain his careful distance.

His heart was a solid block of ice but if it ever started to melt, he knew he couldn't let himself care about Julia Blair and her children. He couldn't afford it.

He had been through enough pain and loss for a hundred lifetimes. He would have to be crazy to sign up for a situation with the potential to promise plenty more.

When he was ready to let people into his life again— if he was ever ready—it couldn't be a medically fragile little girl, a boy with curious eyes and energy to burn, and a lovely auburn-haired widow who made him long to taste life again.

She didn't see Will again for several days. With the lead-up to the start of school and then the actual chaos of adjusting to a new classroom and coming to know thirty new students, she barely had time to give him more than a passing thought.

But twice in the early hours of the morning as she graded math refresher assignments and the obligatory essays about how her students had spent the summer, she had glimpsed the telltale glimmer of lights in his workshop through the pines.

Only the walls of Abigail's old house knew that both

times she had stopped what she was doing to stand at the window for a few moments watching that light and wondering what he was working on, what he was thinking about, if he'd had a good day.

It wasn't obsession, she told herself firmly. Only curiosity about an old friend.

Other than those few silent moments, she hadn't allowed herself to think about him much. What would be the point?

She had seen his reaction to the news of Maddie's cancer, a completely normal response under the circumstances. He had been shocked and saddened and she certainly couldn't blame him for the quick way he distanced himself from her.

She understood, but it still saddened her.

Now, the Friday after school started, she pulled into the Brambleberry House driveway to find his pickup truck parked just ahead of her SUV. Before she could contain the instinctive reaction, her stomach skittered with anticipation.

"Hey, I think that's Mr. Garrett's truck," Simon exclaimed. "See, it says Garrett Construction on the side."

"I think you must be right." She was quite proud of herself for the calm reply.

"I wonder what's he doing here." Simon's voice quivered with excitement and she sighed. Her son was so desperately eager for a man in his life. She couldn't really blame him—except for Conan, who didn't really count, Simon was surrounded by women in every direction.

"Do you think he's working on something for Sage and Anna? Can I help him, do you think? I could hand him tools or something. I'm really good at that. Do you think he'll let me?"

"I don't know the answer to any of your questions, kiddo. You'll have to ask him. Why don't we go check it out?"

Both children jumped out of the vehicle the moment she put it in park. She called to them to wait for her but either they didn't hear her or they chose to ignore her as they rushed to the backyard, where the sound of some kind of power tool hummed through the afternoon.

She caught up with them before they made it all the way.

"I don't want you bothering Will—Mr. Garrett—if he's too busy to answer all your many questions. He has a job to do here and we need to let him."

The rest of what she might have said died in her throat when they turned the corner and she spotted him.

Oh mercy. He wore a pair of disreputable-looking jeans, a forest green T-shirt that bulged with muscle in all the right places, and a leather carpenter's belt slung low like a gunfighter's holster. The afternoon sun picked up golden streaks in his brown hair and he had just a hint of afternoon stubble that made him look dangerous and delectable at the same time.

Oh mercy.

Conan was curled under the shade nearby and his bark of greeting alerted Will's to their presence.

The dog lunged for Simon and Maddie as if he hadn't seen them in months instead of only a few hours and Will even gifted them with a rare smile, there only for an instant before it flickered away.

He drew off his leather gloves and shoved them in the back pocket of his jeans. "School over already? Is it that late?"

"We have early dismissal on Fridays. It's only three o'clock," Julia answered.

"We've been out for a few hours already," Maddie informed him. "Usually we get to stay at the after-school club until Mama finishes her work in her classroom."

"Is that right?"

"It's really fun," Simon answered. "Sometimes we have to stay in Mom's room with her and do our homework if we have a lot, but most of the time we go to extracurriculars. Today we played tetherball and made up a skit and played on the playground for a long time."

"Sounds tiring."

"Not for me," Simon boasted. "Maybe for Maddie."

"I'm not tired," Maddie protested.

His gaze met Julia's in shared acknowledgment that Maddie's claim was obviously a lie.

"What's the project today?" she asked.

"Last time I was here I noticed the back steps were splintering in a few places. I had a couple of hours this afternoon so I decided to get started on replacing them before somebody gets hurt."

Simon looked enthralled. "Can we help you fix them? I could hand you tools and stuff."

That subtle panic sparked in his eyes, the same uneasiness she saw the day they went for ice cream, whenever she or the children had pushed him for more than he was willing to offer.

She could see him trying to figure a way out of the situation without hurting Simon and she quickly stepped in.

"We promised Sage we would pick a bushel of apples and make our famous caramel apple pie, remember? You finally get to meet Chloe in a few hours when she and her father arrive."

Simon scowled. "But you said in the car that if Mr. Garrett said it was okay, we could help him."

She sent a quick look of apology to Will before turning back to her son. "I know, but I could really use your help with the pies."

"Making pies is for girls. I'd rather work with tools and stuff," Simon muttered.

Will raised an eyebrow at this blatantly chauvinistic attitude. "Not true, kid. I know lots of girls who are great at using tools and one of my good friends is a pastry chef at a restaurant down the coast. He makes the best brambleberry pie you'll ever eat in your life."

"Brambleberry, like our house?" Maddie asked.

"Just like."

"Cool!" Simon said. "I want some."

"No brambleberries today," Julia answered. "We're making apple, remember? Let's go change our clothes and get started."

Simon's features drooped with disappointment. "So I don't get to help Mr. Garrett?"

"Simon—"

"I don't mind if he stays and helps," Will said.

"Are you sure?"

He nodded, though she could still see a shadow of reluctance in his eyes. "Positive. I'll enjoy the company. Conan's a good listener but not much of a conversationalist."

She smiled at the unexpected whimsy. "Conversing is one thing Simon does exceptionally well, don't you, kiddo?"

Simon giggled. "Yep. My dad used to say I could talk for a day and a half without needing anybody to answer back."

"I guess that means you probably talk in your sleep, right?"

Simon giggled. "I don't, but Maddie does sometimes. It's really funny. One time she sang the whole alphabet song in her sleep."

"I was only five," Maddie exclaimed to defend herself.

"And you're going to be fifteen before we finish this pie if we don't hurry. We all need to change out of school clothes and into apple-picking and porch-fixing clothes."

Simon looked resigned, then his features brightened. "Race you!" he called to Maddie and took off for the house. She followed several paces behind with Conan barking at their heels, leaving Julia alone with Will.

"I hope he doesn't get in your way or talk your ear off."

"Don't worry. We'll be fine."

"Feel free to send him out to play if you need to."

They lapsed into silence. She should go upstairs, she knew, but she had suddenly discovered she had missed him this last week, silly as that seemed after years when she hadn't given the man a thought.

She couldn't seem to force herself to leave. Finally she sighed, giving into the inevitable.

She took a step closer to him. "Hold still," she murmured.

Wariness leapt into the depths of his blue eyes but he froze as if she had just cast his boots in concrete.

He smelled of leather and wood shavings, and hot, sun-warmed male, a delicious combination, and she wanted to stand there for three or four years and just enjoy it. She brushed her fingers against the blade of his cheekbone, feeling warm male skin.

At her touch, their gazes clashed and the wariness in

his eyes shifted instantly to something else, something raw and wild. An answering tremble stirred inside her and for a moment she forgot what she was doing, her fingers frozen on his skin.

His quick intake of breath dragged her back to reality and she quickly dropped her hand, feeling her own face flame.

"You, um, had a little bit of sawdust on your cheek. I didn't want it to find its way into your eye."

"Thanks." She wasn't sure if it was her imagination or not but his voice sounded decidedly hoarse.

She forced a smile and stepped back, though what she really wanted to do was wrap her arms fiercely around his warm, strong neck and hold on for dear life.

"You're welcome," she managed.

With nothing left to be said, she turned and hurried into the house.

She tried hard to put Will out of her mind as she and Maddie plucked Granny Smith apples off Abigail's tree. She might have found it a bit easier to forget about him if the ladder didn't offer a perfect view of the porch steps he was fixing.

Now she paused, her arm outstretched but the apple she was reaching to grab forgotten as she watched him smile at something Simon said. She couldn't hear them from here but so far it looked as if Simon wasn't making too big a pest of himself.

"Is this enough, Mama?" Maddie asked from below, where she stood waiting by the bushel basket.

Julia jerked her attention back to her daughter and the task at hand. "Just a moment." She plucked three more and added them to the glistening green pile in the basket.

"That ought to do it."

"Do we really need that many apples?"

"Not for one pie but I thought we could make a couple of extras. What do you think?"

She thought for a moment. "Can we give one to Mr. Garrett?"

Maddie looked over at the steps where Simon was trying his hand with Will's big hammer and Julia saw both longing and a sad kind of resignation in her daughter's blue eyes.

Maddie could be remarkably perceptive about others. Julia thought perhaps her long months of treatment—enough to make any child grow up far too early—had sensitized her to the subtle behaviors of others toward her. The way adults tried not to stare after she lost her hair, the stilted efforts of nurses and doctors to befriend her, even Julia's attempts to pretend their world was normal. Maddie seemed to see through them all.

Could Maddie sense the careful distance Will seemed determined to maintain between them?

Julia hoped not. Her daughter had endured enough.

She didn't need more rejection in her life right now when she was just beginning to find her way again.

"That's a good idea," she finally answered Maddie, hoping her smile looked more genuine than it felt. "And perhaps we can think of someone else who might need a pie."

She lifted the bushel and started to carry it around the front of the house. She hadn't made it far before Will stepped forward and took the bushel out of her hands.

"Here, I'll carry that up the stairs for you."

She almost protested that it wasn't necessary but she could tell by the implacable set of his jaw that he wouldn't accept any arguments from her on the matter.

"Thank you," she said instead.

She and Maddie followed him up the stairs.

"Where do you want this?" he asked.

"The kitchen counter by the sink."

"We have to wash every single apple and see if it has a worm," Maddie informed him. "I hope we don't find one. That would be gross."

"That's a lot of work," he said stiffly.

"It is. But my mama's pies are the best. Even better than brambleberry. Just wait until you try one."

Will's gaze flashed to Julia's then away so quickly she wondered if she'd imagined the quick flare of heat there.

"Good luck with your pies."

"Good luck with your stairs," she responded. "Send Simon up if you need to."

He nodded and headed out the door, probably completely oblivious that he was leaving two females to watch wistfully after him.

Chapter Eight

About halfway through helping Julia peel the apples, Maddie asked if she could stop for a few minutes and take a little rest.

"Of course, baby," Julia assured her.

Already Maddie had made it an hour past the time when Julia thought she would give out. School alone was exhausting for her, especially starting at a new school and the effort it took to make new friends. Throw in an hour of after-school activities then picking the apples and it was no wonder Maddie was drooping.

A few moments later, Julia peered through the kitchen doorway to the living room couch and found her curled up, fast asleep.

Julia set down the half-peeled apple, dried her hands off on her apron, and went to double-check on her. Yes, it might be a bit obsessive, but she figured she had earned the right the last few years to a little cautious overreaction.

Maddie's color looked good, though, and she was breathing evenly so Julia simply covered her with her favorite crocheted throw and returned to the kitchen.

Her job was a bit lonely now, without Maddie's quiet observations or Simon's bubbly chatter. With nothing to distract her, she found her gaze slipping with increasing frequency out the window.

She couldn't see much from this angle but every once in awhile Will and Simon would pass into the edge of her view as they moved from Will's power saw to the porch.

She had nearly finished peeling the apples when she suddenly heard a light scratch on the door of her apartment over the steady hammering and the occasional whine of power tools.

Somehow she wasn't surprised to find Conan standing on the other side, his tail wagging and his eyes expectant.

"Let me guess," she murmured. "All that hammering is interfering with your sleep."

She could swear the dog dipped his head up and down as if nodding. He padded through the doorway and into the living room, where he made three circles of his body before easing down to his stomach on the floor beside Maddie's couch.

"Watch over her for me, won't you?"

The dog rested his head on his front paws, his attention trained on Maddie as if the couch where she slept was covered in peanut butter.

"Good boy," Julia murmured, and returned to the kitchen.

She finished her work quickly, slicing enough apples for a half-dozen pies.

She assembled the pies quickly—cheating a little and using store-bought pie shells. She had a good pie crust recipe but she didn't have the time for it today since Eben and Chloe would be returning soon.

Only two pies could cook at a time in her oven and they took nearly forty minutes. After she slid the first pair in, she untied her apron and hung it back on the hook in the kitchen.

Without giving herself time to consider, she grabbed the egg timer off the stovetop, set it for the time the pies needed and stuck it in her pocket, then headed down the stairs to check on Simon.

It was nearly five-thirty but she couldn't see any sign of Anna or Sage yet. Sage, she knew, would be meeting Eben and Chloe at the small airstrip in Seaside, north of Cannon Beach. As for Anna, she sometimes worked late at her store in town or the new one in Lincoln City she had opened earlier in the summer.

She followed the sound of male voices—Will's lower-pitched voice a counterpoint to Simon's mile-a-minute higher tones.

She stepped closer, still out of sight around the corner of the house, until she could hear their words.

"My mom says next year I can play Little League baseball," Simon was saying.

"Hold the board still or we'll have wobbly steps, which won't do anyone any good."

"Sorry."

"Baseball, huh?" Will said a moment later.

"Yep. I couldn't play this year because of Maddie's bone transplant and because we were moving here. But next year, for sure. I can't wait. I played last year, even though I had to miss a lot of games and stuff when Mad was in the hospital."

She closed her eyes, grieving for her son who had suffered right along with his sister. Sometimes it was so easy to focus on Maddie's more immediate needs that she forgot Simon walked each step of the journey right along with her.

"Yeah, I hit six home runs last year. I bet I could do a lot more this year. Did you ever play baseball?"

"Sure did," Will answered. "All through high school and college. Until a few years ago, I was even on a team around here that played in the summertime."

"Probably old guys, huh?"

Julia cringed but Will didn't seem offended, judging by his quick snort of laughter—the most lighthearted sound she had heard from him since she'd been back.

"Yeah. We have a tough time running the bases for all the canes and walkers in the way."

Julia couldn't help herself, she laughed out loud, drawing the attention of both Will and Simon.

"Hi, Mom," Simon chirped, looking pleased to see her. "Guess what? Mr. Garrett played baseball, too."

"I remember," she said. "Your Uncle Charlie dragged me to one of his summer league games the last time I was here and I got to watch him play. He hit a three-run homer."

"Trying to impress you," Will said in a laconic tone.

She laughed again. "It worked very well, as I recall."

That baseball game had been when she first starting thinking of Will as more than just her brother's summer-vacation friend. She hadn't been able to stop thinking about him.

What, exactly, had changed since she came back? she wondered. She still couldn't seem to stop thinking about him.

"My mom likes baseball, too," Simon said. "She said maybe next month sometime we can go to a Mariners game, if they're in the playoffs. It's not very far to Seattle."

His eyes lit up with sudden excitement. "Hey, Mr. Garrett, you could come with us! That would be cool."

Will's gaze met hers and for an instant she imagined sharing hot dogs and listening to the cheers and sitting beside him for three hours, his heat and strength just inches away from her.

"I do enjoy watching the Mariners," Will said, an un-readable look in his eyes. "I'm pretty busy next month but if you let me know when you're going, I can see how it fits my schedule."

"We haven't made any definite plans," Julia said, hoping none of the longing showed in her expression.

She hadn't realized until this moment that Simon wasn't the only one in their family who hungered for a man in their lives.

And not just any man, either. Only a strong, quiet car-penter with callused hands and a rare, beautiful smile.

She decided to quickly change the subject. "The stairs look wonderful. Are you nearly finished?"

Before he could answer, they heard sudden excited barking from the front of the house.

Julia laughed. "I guess Conan needed to go out. It's a good thing he has his own doggy door."

"Hang on a minute," Will said. "That's his *some-body's home* bark."

A moment later they heard a vehicle pull into the driveway.

"Conan!" a high, excited voice shrieked and the dog woofed a greeting.

"That would be Chloe," Will said.

By tacit agreement, the three of them walked together toward the front of the house. When they rounded the corner, Julia saw a dark-haired girl around the twins' age with her arms around the dog's neck.

Beside her, Sage—glowing with joy—stood beside a man with commanding features and brilliant green eyes.

"Hey, guys!" Sage beamed at them. "Julia, this is Chloe Spencer and her dad Eben."

Julia smiled, though she would have known their identities just from the glow on Sage's features—the same one that flickered there whenever she talked about her fiancé and his daughter.

"Eben, this is Julia Blair."

The man offered a smile and his hand to shake. "The new tenant with the twins. Hello. It's a pleasure to meet you finally. Sage has told me a great deal about you and your children the last few weeks."

Sage had told her plenty about Eben and Chloe as well. Meeting them in person, she could well understand how Sage could find the man compelling.

It seemed an odd mix to her—the buttoned-down hotel executive who wore an elegant silk power tie and the free-thinking naturalist who believed her dog communicated with her dead friend. But Julia could tell in an instant they were both crazy about each other.

Eben Spencer turned to Will next and the two of them exchanged greetings. As they spoke, she couldn't help contrasting the two men. Though Eben was probably more classically handsome in a *GQ* kind of way, with his loosened tie and his rolled up shirt sleeves, she had to admit that Will's toolbelt and worn jeans affected her more.

Being near Eben Spencer didn't make her insides flutter and her bones turn liquid.

"And who's this?" Eben was asking, she realized when she jerked her attention back to the conversation.

Color soaked her cheeks and she hoped no one else noticed. "This is one of my kiddos. Simon, this is Mr. Spencer and his daughter Chloe."

"I'm eight," Chloe announced. "How old are you?"

Simon immediately went into defensive mode. "Well," he said slowly, "I won't be eight until March. But I'm taller than you are."

Chloe made a face. "*Everyone* is taller than me. I'm a shrimp. Sage says you have a twin sister. How cool! Where is she?"

He looked to Julia for an answer.

"Upstairs," she answered. "I'll go wake her, though. She's been anxious to meet you."

As if on cue, her timer beeped. "Got to run. That would be my pies ready to come out of the oven."

"You're making pie?" Chloe exclaimed. "That's super cool. I just *love* pie."

She smiled, charmed by Sage's stepdaughter-to-be. "I do, too. But not burnt pie so I'd better hurry."

She tried to be quiet as she slid the pies from the oven and carefully set them on a rack to dry, but she must have clattered something because Maddie began to stir in the other room.

She stood in the doorway and watched her daughter

rise to a sitting position on the couch. "Hey, baby. How are you feeling?"

Maddie gave an ear-popping yawn and stretched her arms above her head. "Pretty good. I'm sorry, Mama. I said I would help you make pies and then I fell asleep."

"You helped me with the hard part, which was picking the apples and washing them all."

"I guess."

She still looked dejected at her own limitations and Julia walked to her and pulled her into a hug. "You helped me a ton. I never would have been able to finish without you. And while you were sleeping soundly, guess who arrived?"

Her features immediately brightened. "Chloe?"

"Yep. She's outside with Simon right now."

"Can I go meet her?"

She smiled at her enthusiasm. One thing about Maddie, even in the midst of her worst fatigue, she could go from full sleep to complete alertness in a matter of seconds.

"Of course. Go ahead. I'll be down in a minute—I just have to put in these other pies."

A few moments later, she closed her apartment door and headed down the stairs. The elusive scent of freesia seemed to linger in the air and she wondered if that was Abigail's way of greeting the newcomers. The whimsical thought had barely registered when Anna's door—Abigail's old apartment—slowly opened.

She instinctively gasped, then flushed crimson when Will walked out, a measuring tape in hand.

What had she expected? The ghostly specter of Abigail, complete with flashy costume jewelry and a wicked smile?

"Hi," she managed.

He gave her an odd look. "Everything okay?"

"Yes. Just my imagination running away with me."

"I was double-checking the measurements for the new moldings in Anna's apartment. I'm hoping to get to them in a week or so."

"All done with the stairs, then?"

"Not quite. I'm still going to have to stain them but the bulk of the hard work is done."

"You do good work, Will. I'm very impressed."

"My dad taught me well."

The scent of freesia seemed stronger now and finally she had to say something. "Okay, tell me something. Can you smell that?"

Confusion flickered across his rugged features. "I smell sawdust and your apple pie baking. That's it."

"You don't smell freesia?"

"I'm not sure I know what that is."

"It's a flower. Kind of light, delicate. Abigail used to wear freesia perfume, apparently. I don't remember that about her but Anna and Sage say she did and I believe them."

He still looked confused. "And you're smelling it now?"

She sighed, knowing she must sound ridiculous. "Sage thinks Abigail is sticking around Brambleberry House. "

To her surprise, he laughed out loud and she stared, arrested by the sound. "I wouldn't put it past her," he said. "She loved this old place."

"I can't say I blame her for that. I'm coming to love it, too. There's a kind of peace here—I can't explain it. Maddie says the house is friendly and I have to tell you, I'm beginning to believe her."

He shook his head, but he was smiling. "Watch out or you'll turn as wacky as Sage. Next thing I know, you'll be balancing your chakras every five minutes and eating only tofu and bean sprouts."

She gazed at his smile for a long moment, arrested by his light-hearted expression. He looked young and much more relaxed than she had seen him in a long time, almost happy, and her heart rejoiced that she had been able to make him smile and, yes, even laugh.

His smile slid away after a moment and she realized she was staring at his mouth. She couldn't seem to look away, suddenly wildly curious to know what it would be like to kiss him again.

Something hot kindled in the blue of his eyes and she caught her breath, wanting his touch, his kiss, more than she had wanted anything in a long time.

He wasn't ready, she reminded herself, and eased back, sliding her gaze from his. No sooner had she made up her mind to step away and let the intense moment pass when she could swear she felt a determined hand between her shoulderblades, pushing her forward.

She whirled around in astonishment, then thought she must be going crazy. Only the empty stairs were behind her.

"What's wrong?" Will asked. Though his words were concerned, that stony, unapproachable look had returned to his expression and she sighed, already missing that brief instant of laughter.

"Um, nothing. Absolutely nothing. My imagination seems to be in overdrive, that's all."

"That's what you get for talking about ghosts."

She forced a smile and headed for the for door. Just before she walked through it, she turned and aimed a glare at the empty room.

Stay out of my love life, Abigail, she thought. *Or any lack thereof.*

She could almost swear wicked laughter followed behind her.

Damn it. He wasn't at all ready for this.

Will followed Julia out the door, still aware of the heat and hunger simmering through him.

He had almost kissed her. The urge had been so strong, he had been only seconds away from reaching for her.

She wouldn't have stopped him. He sensed that much—he had seen the warm welcome in her eyes and had known she would have returned the kiss with enthusiasm.

He still didn't know why he had stopped or why she had leaned away then looked behind her as if fearing her children were skulking on the second-floor landing watching them.

He didn't know why they hadn't kissed but he was enormously grateful they had both come to their senses.

He didn't want to be attracted to another woman. Sure, he was a man and he had normal needs just like any other male. But he had been crazy about his wife. Kissing another woman—even *wanting* to kiss another woman—still seemed like some kind of betrayal, though intellectually he knew that was absurd.

Robin had been gone for more than two years. As much as he had loved her, he sometimes had to work hard to summon the particular arrangement of her features and the sound of her voice.

He was forgetting her and he hated it. Sometimes his grief seemed like a vast lake that had been frozen solid forever. Suddenly, as if overnight, the ice was beginning to crack around the edges. He wouldn't have expected it to hurt like hell but everything suddenly seemed more raw than it had since the accident.

He pressed his fist to the ache in chest for just a moment then headed for the backyard, where he had set up his power tools. His gaze seemed to immediately drift to Julia and he found her on the brick patio, laughing at something Sage had said, the afternoon sunlight finding gold strands in her hair. He could swear he felt more chunks of ice break free.

She must have sensed the weight of his stare—she turned her head slightly and their gazes collided for a brief moment before he broke the connection and picked up his power saw and headed for his truck.

On his next trip to get the sawhorses, he deliberately forced himself not to look at her. He was so busy *not* looking at her that he nearly mowed down Eben.

"Sorry," he muttered, feeling like an ass.

Eben laughed. "No problem. You look like your mind's a million miles away."

He judged her to be only about twenty-five feet, but he wasn't going to quibble. "Something like that," he murmured.

He hadn't expected to like Eben Spencer. When Sage had first fallen for the man, Will had been quite certain he would break her heart. As he had come to know him these last few months, he had changed his mind. Eben was deeply in love with Sage.

The two of them belonged together in a way Will couldn't have explained to save his life.

"You look like you could use a hand clearing this up."

He raised an eyebrow. "No offense, but you're not really dressed for moving my grimy tools."

"I don't mind getting a little dirty once in a while." The other man hefted two sawhorses over one shoulder, leaving Will only his toolbox to carry.

"Thanks," he said when everything had been slid into the bed of his pickup truck.

"No problem," Eben said again. "You're staying for dinner, aren't you? Sage has decided to throw an impromptu party since Chloe and I are back in town for a few days. I really don't want to be the only thing around here with a Y chromosome. Beautiful as all these Brambleberry women are, they're a little overwhelming for one solitary man."

"Don't forget you've got Simon Blair around now."

Eben laughed. "Well, that does help even the scales a little, but I have a feeling Sage and the others will be lost in wedding plans. I wouldn't mind company while I'm manning the grill."

He was tempted. He knew he shouldn't be but his empty house had become so oppressive sometimes he hated walking inside it.

"Got anything besides veggie burgers?"

"Sage talked to Jade and Stanley and they're sending over some choice prime-cut steaks from The Sea Urchin—the kind you can't buy at your average neighborhood grocery store."

"Sage *must* be in love if she's chasing down steaks for you," Will said, earning a chuckle from Eben.

"She might be a vegetarian but she's very forgiving of those of us who aren't quite as enlightened yet."

"Maybe she's just biding her time until you're married, then she'll start substituting your bacon for veggie strips and your hamburgers for mushroom, bean-curd concoctions."

Eben smiled, his expression rueful. "I'm so crazy about her, I probably wouldn't mind." He paused. "Stay, why don't you? Anna and Sage would love to have you."

What about Julia? He wondered. His attention shifted to her and that longing came out of nowhere again, knocking him out at the knees.

"Sure," he said, before he could give himself a chance to reconsider. "I just need to run home and wash off some of this sweat and sawdust."

"Great. We'll see you in a few minutes then."

He drove away, already regretting the momentary impulse to accept the invitation.

Chapter Nine

An hour later, after taking a quick shower and changing his clothes, Will stood beside Eben at the grill, beer in hand, asking himself again why he had possibly thought this might be a good idea.

It was a lovely evening, he had to admit that. A breeze blew off the ocean, cool enough to be refreshing but not cold enough to have anybody reaching for a sweater.

The sweet sound of children's laughter rang through the Brambleberry House yard as Chloe and the twins threw a ball for Conan. Sage, Julia and Anna were sitting at a table on the weathered brick patio looking over wedding magazines.

Abigail would have adored seeing those she loved

most enjoying themselves together. This casual, informal kind of gathering was exactly the kind of thing she loved best.

He only wished he could enjoy himself as he used to do, that he didn't view the whole scene with his chest aching and this deep sense of loss in his gut.

"My people at The Sea Urchin tell me the work you've done on the new cabinetry in the lobby is spectacular," Eben said as he turned the steaks one last time.

Will forced a smile. "I had great bones to work with. That helps on any project."

"She's a beautiful old place, isn't she?" Eben's smile was much more genuine. "I'm sorry I haven't had the opportunity yet to see what you've accomplished there. I'm looking forward to tomorrow when I have a chance to check out the progress of the last three weeks while Chloe and I have been overseas. I've been getting daily reports but it's not the same as seeing it firsthand."

"I think you'll be happy with it. You've got some real craftsmen working on The Sea Urchin."

"Including you." He took a sip of his beer, then gave Will an intent look. "In fact, I've got a proposition for you."

Will raised an eyebrow, curiosity replacing the ache, if only temporarily. Another job? he wondered. As far as he knew, The Sea Urchin was the only Spencer Hotels property along the coast.

"Spencer Hotels could always use a master carpenter. We've got rehab projects going in eight different properties right now alone. There's always something popping. What would you say to signing on with us, traveling a little? You could take your pick of the jobs, anywhere from Tokyo to Tuscany. We've got more than enough work to keep you busy, with much more in the pipeline."

He blinked, stunned at the offer. He was just a journeyman carpenter in piddly little Cannon Beach. What the hell did he know about either Tokyo or Tuscany?

"Whoa," he finally managed through his shock. "That's certainly…unexpected."

"I've been thinking about it for awhile. When I received the glowing report from my people here, it just seemed a confirmation of what had already been running around my head. I think you'd be perfect for the job. I usually try to hire workers from the various communities where my hotels are located—good business practice, you know—but I also like to have my own man overseeing the work."

"I don't know what good I would be in that capacity. I don't speak any language except good old English and a little bit of Spanish."

"The Spanish might help. But we always have translators on site, so that's not really a concern. I'm looking for a craftsman. An artisan. From what I've seen of your work, you definitely qualify. I also want someone I can trust to do the job right. And again, you qualify."

He had to admit, he was flattered. How could he not be? He loved his work and took great pride in it. When others saw and acknowledged a job well done, he found enormous satisfaction.

For just a moment, he allowed himself to imagine the possibilities. He had lived his entire life in Cannon Beach—in the very same house, even. Though he loved the town and loved living on the coast, maybe it was time to pick up and try something new, see the world a little.

On the other hand. he wasn't sure the ghosts that haunted him were ready for him to move on.

"You don't have to give me any kind of answer tonight," Eben said at his continued silence. "Just think about it. If you decide you're interested, we can sit down while I'm here and talk details."

"I'll think about it," he agreed. "I…it's a little over-whelming. It would be a huge change for me."

"But maybe not an unwelcome one," Eben said, showing more insight than Will was completely com-fortable with.

"Maybe not." He paused. "I've got a buddy up in Ketchikan who's been after me to come up and go into business with him. I've been tossing the idea around."

"That might be good for you, too. Look at all your options. Take all the time you need. As far as I'm con-cerned, you can consider the Spencer Hotels offer an in-definite one with no time limit."

"What offer?"

He hadn't even noticed Sage had joined them until she

spoke. Now she slipped her arm through the crook of Will's elbow and gave his arm an affectionate squeeze. Of all his friends, Sage was the most physical, and he always appreciated her hugs and kisses on the cheek and the times, like now, when she squeezed his arm.

He didn't like to admit it, but he sometimes ached for the soft comfort of a woman's touch, even the touch of a woman he considered more in the nature of a little sister than anything else.

"You won't like it," Eben predicted.

She made a face. "Try me. Believe it or not, I can be remarkably open-minded sometimes."

"Good. It might be a good idea for you to keep that in mind," Eben said with a wary expression.

"What are you up to?"

"I'm trying to steal Will away from Cannon Beach to come work for Spencer Hotels."

She dropped her arm and glared with shock at both of them. "You can't leave! We need you here."

"Says the woman who's going to be moving to San Francisco herself in a few months," Will murmured.

She tucked a loose strand of wavy blonde hair behind her ear, flushing a little at the reminder. "Not full-time. We'll be here every summer so I can still run the nature center camps. And we're planning to spend as much time up here as we can—weekends and school holidays."

"But you'll still be in the Bay Area most of the time, right?"

"Yes." She made a face. "I'm selfish, I know. I just don't want things to change."

"Things change, Sage. Most of the time we have no choice but to change, too, whether we want to or not."

She squeezed his arm again, her eyes suddenly moist. He saw memories of Robin and Cara swimming there and he didn't want to ruin her night by bringing up the past.

"I'm not going anywhere right now," he said. "Let's just enjoy the evening while we can."

Eben kissed his fiancée on the tip of her nose, an intimate gesture that for some reason made Will's chest ache. "These steaks are just about ready and I think your bean burger is perfect, though I believe that statement is a blatant oxymoron."

She laughed and headed off to tell the others dinner was ready.

"Give my offer some thought," Eben said when Sage was out of earshot. "Like I said, you don't have to answer right away. Maybe you could try it for six months or so to see how the traveling lifestyle fits you."

"I'll think about it," he agreed, which was an understatement of major proportions.

They ate on the brick patio, protected from the wind blowing off the sea by the long wall of Sitka spruce on the seaward edge of the yard.

While he and Eben had been grilling, the women had set out candles of varying heights around the patio and turned on the little twinkling fairy lights he had hung in the trees for Abigail a few summers earlier.

It seemed an odd collection of people but somehow the mix worked. Sage, with her highly developed social conscience. Anna with her quiet ambition and hard work ethic. Eben, dynamic businessman, and Julia, warm and nurturing, making sure plates were full, that the potato salad was seasoned just so, that drinks were replenished.

A group of very different people brought together because of Abigail, really.

Conversation flowed around him like an incoming tide finding small hidden channels in the sand and he was mostly content to sit at the table and listen to it.

"You're not eating your steak."

He looked up to find Julia watching him, her green eyes concerned. Though she sat beside him, he hadn't been ignoring her for the last hour but he hadn't exactly made any effort to seek her out, still disconcerted by that moment in the hallway when he had wanted to kiss her more than he wanted oxygen.

Sorry," he mumbled and immediately applied himself to the delicious cut in front of him.

"You don't have to eat it just because I said something." She pitched her voice low so others didn't overhear. "I was just wondering if everything is okay. You seem distracted."

He was distracted by *her*. By the cherry blossom scent of her, and her softness so close to him and the inappropriate thoughts he couldn't seem to shake.

"You don't know me anymore, Julia. For all you know, maybe I'm always this way."

As soon as the sharp words left his mouth, a cold wind suddenly forced its way past the line of trees to flutter the edges of the tablecloth and send the lights shivering in the treetops.

He didn't miss the hurt that leapt into her eyes or the way her mouth tightened.

He was immediately contrite. "I'm sorry. I'm not really fit company tonight."

"No, you're not. But it happens to all of us." She turned away to talk to Eben, on her other side, and the prime-cut steak suddenly had all the appeal of overdried beef jerky.

He would have to do a better job of apologizing for his sharp words, he realized. She didn't deserve to bear the brunt of his temper.

His chance didn't come until sometime later when everyone seemed to have finished dinner. Julia stood and started clearing dishes and Will immediately rose to help her, earning a surprised look and even a tentative smile from her.

"Where are we taking all this stuff?" he asked when he had an armload of dishes.

"My apartment. My dishwasher is the newest and the biggest. Most of the dishes came out of my kitchen anyway and I can make sure those that belong to Sage or Anna are returned to their rightful homes."

He followed her up the stairs, then headed down for

another load. When he returned, she was rinsing and loading dishes in the dishwasher and he immediately started helping.

She flashed him one quick, questioning look, then smiled and made room for him at the sink.

The sheer domesticity of it stirred that same weird ache in his throat and he could feel himself wanting to shut down, to flee to the safety and empty solitude of his house down the beach.

But he had come this far. He could tough it out a little longer.

"I owe you an apology for my sharpness," he said after a moment. "A better one than the sorry excuse I gave you outside."

Her gaze collided with his for just a moment before she returned her attention to the sink. "You don't owe me anything, Will. I overstepped and I'm sorry. I've been overstepping since I came back to Cannon Beach."

She sighed and turned around, her hip leaning against the sink. "You were absolutely right, we don't have any kind of…anything. We were friends a long time ago, when we were both vastly different people. That was in the past. Somehow I keep forgetting that today we're simply two people who happen to live a few houses apart and have the same circle of friends."

"That's not quite true."

She frowned. "Which part isn't true?"

"That we were friends so long ago."

Hurt flickered in her eyes but she quickly concealed it and turned back to the sink. "My mistake, then. I guess you're right. We didn't know each other well. Just a few weeks every summer."

He should just stop now before he made things worse. What was the point in dragging all this up again?

"That's not what I meant. I only meant that the way we left things was definitely more than just friends."

She stared at him, sudden awareness blossoming in the green of her eyes.

"It took me a long time to get over you," he said, and the admission looked as if it surprised her as much as it did him. "When you didn't answer my letters, I figured everything I thought we had was all in my head. But it still hurt."

"Oh, Will." She dried her hands on a dish towel. "I would have written you but…things were so messed up. I was messed up. The day we returned home from our last summer in Cannon Beach, my parents told us they were divorcing. This was only two weeks before school started. My dad ended up with Charlie and the house in Los Angeles, and my mom took me to Sacramento with her. I had to start a new school my junior year, which was terrible. I didn't even get your letters until almost the end of the school year when my dad finally bothered to forward them from L.A."

She touched his arm, much the way Sage had earlier,

but Sage's touch hadn't given him instant goosebumps or make him want to yank her into his arms.

"I should have written to explain to you what was going on," she went on. "I'm sorry I didn't, but I never forgot you, Will. This probably sounds really stupid, but the time I spent with you that summer was the best thing that happened to me in a long time, either before it or after, and I didn't want to spoil the memory of it."

She smiled, her hand still on his arm. He was dying here and he doubted she even realized what effect she was having on him. "You have no idea how long it took me to stop comparing every other boy to you."

"What can I say? I'm a hell of a kisser."

He meant the words as a flippant joke and she gave him a startled laugh, then followed up with a sidelong glance. "I do believe I remember that about you," she murmured.

The intimacy of the room seemed to wrap around them. For one wild moment, he felt sixteen again, lost in the throes of first love, entranced by Julia Hudson.

He could kiss her.

The impulse to taste her, touch her, poured through him and he was powerless to fight it. He took a step forward, expecting her to back away. Instead, her gaze locked with his and he saw in her eyes an awareness—even a longing—to match his own.

Still he hesitated, the only sound in the kitchen their mingled breathing. He might have stayed in an eternity of indecision if she hadn't leaned toward him slightly, just enough to tumble the last of his defenses.

In an instant, his mouth found hers and captured her quick gasp of surprise.

So long. So damn long.

He had forgotten how soft a woman's mouth could be, how instantly addictive it could be to taste desire.

Part of him wanted to yank back and retreat to his frozen lake where he was safe. But he was helpless to fight the tide of yearning crashing over him, the heat and sensation and pure, delicious pleasure of her softness against him.

It seemed impossible, but he tasted better than she remembered, of cinnamon and mint and coffee.

She should be shocked that he would kiss her, after being quite blunt that he wasn't interested in starting anything. But it seemed so right to be here in his arms that she couldn't manage to summon anything but grateful amazement.

She slid her arms around his neck, letting him set the pace and tone of the kiss. It was gentle at first, sweet and comfortable. Two old friends renewing something they had once shared.

Just as it had so many years earlier, being in his arms felt right. Completely perfect.

Their bodies had changed over the years—he was much broader and more muscled and she knew giving birth to twins had softened her edges and given her more curves.

But they still seemed to fit together like two halves of the same planed board.

She was aware of odd, random sensations as the kiss lingered—the hard countertop digging into her hip where he pressed her against it, the silk of his hair against her fingers, the smell of him, leathery and masculine.

And freesia.

The smell of flowers drifted through her kitchen so strongly that she opened one eye to make sure Abigail wasn't standing in the doorway watching them.

An instant later, she forgot all about Abigail—or any other ghosts—when Will pulled her closer and deepened the kiss, his tongue playing and teasing in a way that demonstrated quite unequivocally that he had learned more than a few things in the intervening years since their last kiss on the beach.

Heat flared, bright and urgent, and she dived right into the flames, holding him closer and returning the kiss.

She had no idea how long they kissed—or just how long they might have continued. Both of them froze when they heard the squeak of the entry door downstairs.

Will wrenched his mouth away, breathing hard, and stared at her and her heart broke at the expression on his face—shock and dismay and something close to anguish.

He raked a hand through his hair, leaving little tufts looking as if he'd just walked into a wind tunnel.

"That was… I shouldn't have…"

He seemed so genuinely upset, she locked away her hurt and focused on trying to ease his turmoil. "Will, it's okay."

"No. No, it's not. I shouldn't have done that. I've… I've got to go."

Without another word, he hurried out of the kitchen and her apartment and she heard the thud of his boots as he rushed down the wooden stairway and out the door.

She leaned against the counter, her breathing still ragged. She felt emotionally ravaged, wrung out and hung to dry.

She was still trying to figure out what just happened when she heard a knock on her door.

She wasn't sure she was at all ready to face anyone but when the knock sounded again, she knew she wouldn't be able to hide away there in her kitchen forever.

"It's open," she called.

The door swung open and a moment later Anna Galvez walked into the apartment.

"What's up with Will? He passed me on the stairs and didn't even say a word before he headed out the door like the hounds of hell were nipping at his heels."

She gave Julia a careful look. "Are you okay? You look flushed. Did you and Will have a fight or something?"

"That blasted *or something* will get you every time," Julia muttered under her breath.

"You're going to have to give me a break here. I've been working all day on inventory and my brain is mush. Do you want to explain what that means?"

"Not really." She sighed, not at all comfortable talking about this. But right now she desperately needed a friend and Anna definitely qualified. "He kissed me," she blurted out.

Surprise then delight flickered across Anna's features. "Really? That's wonderful!"

"Is it? Will obviously didn't think so."

"Will doesn't do anything he doesn't want to do. If he hadn't wanted to kiss you, he wouldn't have."

"He was horrified afterward."

"A little overdramatic, don't you think?"

"You should have seen his face! I don't think he's ready. He's lost so much."

"So have you. I don't hear you saying you're not ready."

But their situations were vastly different, a point she wasn't prepared to point out to Anna. Will had been happily married when his wife died. She, on the other hand, had let Kevin go long before his fatal car accident.

"He will figure things out in his own time. Don't worry," Anna went on. "He's a wonderful man who's been through a terrible tragedy. But he'll get through it. Have a little faith."

Right now faith was something Julia had in very short supply. She could tumble hard and fast for Will Garrett. It wouldn't take a hard push—she had been in love with him when she was fifteen years old and she could easily see herself falling again.

But what would be the point, if he had his heart so tightly wrapped in protective layers that he wouldn't let anyone in?

Chapter Ten

It was just a damn kiss.

Three weeks later, Will backed his truck into the Brambleberry House driveway, fighting a mix of dread and unwilling anticipation.

He knew both reactions were completely ridiculous. What the hell was he worrying about? She wouldn't even be here—he had finally managed to work the molding job into his schedule only after squeezing in a time when he could be certain Julia and her children were safely tucked away at the elementary school.

The very fact that he had to resort to such ridiculous manipulations of his own schedule simply to avoid seeing a certain woman bugged the heck out of him.

He ought to be tougher than this. He should have been completely unfazed by their brief encounter, instead of brooding about it for the better part of three weeks.

So he had kissed her. Big deal. The world hadn't stopped spinning, the ocean hadn't suddenly been sucked dry, the Coast Range hadn't suddenly tumbled to dust.

Robin hadn't come back to haunt him.

He knew his reaction to the kiss had been excessive. He had run out of her apartment at Brambleberry House like a kid who had been caught smoking in the boy's room of the schoolhouse.

Yeah, he had overreacted to the shock of discovering not all of him was encased in ice—that he could desire another woman, could long to have her wrapped around him.

He still wanted it. That was what had bothered him for three weeks. Even though he hadn't seen her in all that time, she hadn't been far from his thoughts.

He remembered the taste of her, sweet and welcoming, the softness of her skin under his fingers, the subtle peace he had so briefly savored.

He couldn't seem to shake this achy sense that with that single kiss, everything in his world had changed, in a way he couldn't explain but knew he didn't like.

He didn't want change. Yeah, he hated his life and missed Robin and Cara so much he sometimes couldn't breathe around the pain. But it was *his* pain.

He was used to it now, and somewhere deep inside,

he worried that letting go of that grief would mean letting go of his wife and baby girl, something he wasn't ready to face yet.

He knew his reaction was absurd. Plenty of people had lost loved ones and had moved ahead with their lives. His own mother had married again, just a few years after his father died, when Will was in his early twenties. She had moved to San Diego with her new husband, where the two of them seemed to be extremely happy together. They played golf, they went sailing on the bay, they enjoyed an active social life.

Will didn't begrudge his mother her happiness. He liked his stepfather and was grateful his mother had found someone else.

Intellectually, he knew it was possible, even expected, for him to date again sometime. He just wasn't sure he was ready yet—indeed, that he would ever be ready.

It had just been a kiss, he reminded himself. Not a damn marriage proposal.

As he sat in the driveway, gearing himself to go inside, the moist sea breeze drifted through his cracked window and he could suddenly swear he smelled cherry blossoms.

It was nearing the end of September, for heaven's sake, and was a cool, damp morning. He had absolutely no business smelling the spring scent of cherry blossoms on the breeze.

No doubt it was only the power of suggestion at

work—he was thinking about Julia and his subconscious somehow managed to conjure the scent that always seemed to cling to her.

He closed his eyes and for just a moment allowed his mind to wander over that kiss again—the way she had responded to him with such warm enthusiasm, the silky softness of her mouth, the comfort of her hands against his skin.

Just a damn kiss!

His sigh filled the cab of the pickup and he stiffened his resolve and reached for the door handle.

Enough. Anna and Sage weren't paying him to sit on his butt and moon over their tenant. He had work to do. He'd been promising Anna for weeks he would get to her moldings and he couldn't keep putting it off.

A Garrett man kept his promises.

He climbed out and strapped on his tool belt with a dogged determination he would have found amusing under other circumstances, then grabbed as many of the moldings out of the back as he could lift.

He carried them to the porch and set them as close to the house as he could, then went back to his pickup for the rest. Judging by the steely clouds overhead, they were in for rain soon and he needed to keep the custom-cut oak dry.

He nearly dropped his second load when the front door suddenly swung open. A second later, Conan bounded through and barked with excitement.

He set the wood down with the other pile and gave the dog the obligatory scratch. "You're opening the door by yourself now? Pretty soon you're going to be driving yourself to the store to pick up dog food. You won't need any of us anymore."

"Until that amazing day arrives, he'll continue to keep us all as willing slaves. Hi, Will."

His entire insides had clenched at the sound of that first word spoken in a low, musical voice, and he slowly lifted his gaze to find Julia standing in the doorway.

She looked beautiful, fresh and lovely, and he could almost feel the churn of his heart.

"What are you doing here?" he said abruptly. "I figured you'd be at school."

Too late, he realized all that his words revealed—that he had given her more than a minute's thought in the last three weeks. She wasn't a stupid woman. No doubt she would quickly read between the lines and figure out he had purposely planned the project for a time when he was unlikely to encounter her.

To his vast relief, she didn't seem to notice. "I should be. At school, I mean. But Maddie's caught some kind of a bug. She was running a fever this morning and I decided I had better stay home and keep an eye on her."

"Is it a problem, missing your class?"

She shook her head. "I hate having to bring in a substitute this early in the school year but it can't be helped. The school district knew when they hired me that my daughter's health was fragile. So far they've been amazingly cooperative."

"She's okay, isn't she?"

All he could think about even as he asked the question was the irony of the whole thing. Above all else, he had tried his best to avoid bumping into her. So how, in heaven's name, had he managed to pick the one day she was home to finish the job?

"I think she's only caught a little cold," Julia answered. "At least that's what I hope it is. She's sniffly and coughing a bit but her fever broke about an hour ago. I hope it's just one of those twenty-four hour bugs."

"That's good."

"Her night was a little unsettled but she's sleeping soundly now. I figured rest was the best thing for her so I'm letting her sleep as long as she needs to beat this thing."

"Sounds like a smart plan."

"I guess you're here to do the moldings in Anna's apartment."

He nodded curtly, not knowing what else to say.

"Do you have more supplies in your truck that need to come in? I can help you carry things."

"This is it." His voice was more brusque than he intended and Conan made a snarly kind of growl at him.

Will just barely managed not to snarl back. He didn't need a dog making him feel guilty. He could do that all on his own.

It wasn't Julia's fault she stirred all kinds of unwelcome feelings in him and it wasn't at all fair of him to take out his bad mood on her.

He forced himself to temper his tone. "Would you mind holding the door open for me, though? It's going to rain soon and I'd hate for all this oak to get wet."

"Oh! Of course." She hurried to open the door. The only tricky part now was that he would have to move past her to get inside, he realized. He should have considered that little detail.

Too late now.

He let out a sigh of defeat and picked up several of the moldings and squeezed past her, doing his best not to bang the wood on the doorway on his way inside.

Going in wasn't so tough. Walking back out for a second load with his arms unencumbered was an entirely different story. He was painfully aware of her—that scent of spring, the heat of her body, the flicker of awareness in her green eyes as he passed.

Oh, he was in trouble.

His only consolation was that she seemed just as disconcerted by his presence.

"I guess you probably have a key to Anna's apartment, don't you?" she asked.

He nodded. "I have keys to the whole house so I can come and go when I'm working on something. All but your apartment. I gave it back to Anna and Sage when I finished up on the second floor."

"Good to know," she murmured.

He cleared his throat, set down the moldings in the entry and fished in his pocket, then pulled out the Brambleberry keyring. Of course, his hands seemed to fumble as he tried to find the right one to fit the lock for Anna's apartment, but he finally located it and opened her door.

"Would you mind holding the apartment door open as well? I need to be careful not to hit the wood on the frame. If you could guide it through, that would be great."

"Sure!" She hurried to prop open the door with an eagerness that made him blink. Even though it was akin to torture, he had to walk past her all over again and he forced himself to put away this sizzle of awareness and focus on the job.

She followed him inside as he carried the eight-foot-long moldings in and set them behind Anna's couch.

"Can I give you a hand with anything else?" Julia asked. "To be honest, I'm a bit at loose ends this morning and was looking for a distraction. I've already finished my lesson plans for the next month and I'm completely caught up with my homework grading. I was just contemplating rearranging my kitchen cabinets in alphabetical order, just to kill the boredom. I'd love the chance to do something constructive."

That was just about the last thing on earth he needed right now, to have to work with Julia looking on. She was the very definition of distraction. With his luck, he'd probably be so busy trying not to smell her that he would glue his sleeve to the wood.

His hesitation dragged on just a moment too long, he realized as he watched heat soak her cheeks.

"You're used to working alone and I would probably only get in the way, wouldn't I? Forget I said anything."

He hated her distress, hated making her think he didn't want her around. Was he a coward or was he a man who could contain his own unwanted desires?

"I *am* used to working alone," he said slowly, already regretting the words. "But I guess I wouldn't mind the company."

It was almost worth his impending discomfort to see her face light up with such delight. She must really be bored if she could get so excited about handing him tools and watching him nail up moldings.

"I'll just run up and grab the walkie-talkie I let the kids use when they're sick to call out to me when they need drinks and things. That way Maddie will be able to find me when she wakes up."

He nodded, though she didn't seem to expect much of an answer as she hurried out the door and up the stairs.

What the hell had he just done? he wondered. The whole point of scheduling this project during this time had been to avoid bumping into her. He certainly didn't expect to find himself inviting her to spend the next hour or so right next to him, crowding his space, posing far too much of a temptation for his peace of mind.

"What are you grinning at?" he growled to Conan.

The dog just woofed at him and settled onto the rug in front of the empty fireplace. When Abigail was alive, that had always been his favorite place, Will remembered.

He supposed it was nice to see a few things didn't change, even though he felt as if the rest of his life was a deck of cards that had suddenly been thrown into the teeth of the wind.

She was a fool when it came to Will Garrett.

Up in her apartment, Julia quickly ran a brush through her hair. She thought about touching up the quick makeup job she'd done that morning but she figured Will would probably notice—and wonder—if she put on fresh lipstick.

Would he really notice? The snide voice in her head asked. He had made it plain he wasn't interested in her. Or at least that he didn't want to be interested in her, which amounted to the same thing.

More reason she was a fool for Will Garrett. Some part of her held out some foolish hope that this time might be different, that this time he might be able to see beyond the past.

Her conversation with Anna seemed to play through her head again. *He's a wonderful man who's been through a terrible tragedy. But he'll get through it. Have a little faith.*

She understood grief. Understood and accepted it. Despite their marital problems toward the end, she had mourned Kevin's death for the children's sake and for the sake of all those dreams they had once shared, the dreams that had been lost along the way somewhere.

She understood Will's sorrow. But she also accepted that she had missed him these last few weeks.

He hadn't been far from her thoughts, even as she went about the business of living—settling into the school year, getting to know her new students and co-workers at the elementary school, helping Simon and Maddie with their schoolwork.

She glanced out the window at his workshop, tucked away behind his house beneath the trees. How many nights had she stood at the window, watching the lights flicker there, wondering how he was, what he was thinking, what he might be working on?

She was obsessed with the man. Pure and simple. Perhaps they would both be better off if she just stayed up here with her daughter and pushed thoughts of him out of her head.

She sighed. She wasn't going to, because of that whole being-a-fool thing again. She couldn't resist this chance to talk to him again, to indulge herself with his company and perhaps come to know a little more about the man he had become.

She opened Maddie's door and found her daughter still sleeping, her skin a healthy color and her breathing even. Julia scribbled a quick note to tell her where she was.

"I have the other walkie-talkie so just let me know

when you wake up," she wrote and slipped the note under the other wireless handset on Maddie's bedside table where she couldn't miss it.

She spent one more moment watching the miracle of her daughter sleeping.

It was exactly the reminder she needed to wake her to the harsh reality of just how cautious she needed to be around Will Garrett.

Girlhood crushes were one thing, but she had two children to worry about now. She couldn't risk their feelings, couldn't let them come to care any more about a man who quite plainly wasn't ready to let anyone else into his life.

She would walk downstairs and be friendly in a polite, completely casual way, she told herself as she headed for the door. She wouldn't push him, she wouldn't dig too deeply.

She would simply help him with his project and try to bridge the tension between them so they could remain on friendly terms.

Anything else would be beyond foolish, when she had her children's emotional well-being to consider.

Chapter Eleven

When she returned to Anna's apartment, she found Conan sleeping on his favorite rug but no sign of Will. His tools and the boards he had brought in were still in evidence but Will wasn't anywhere to be found so Julia settled down to wait.

A moment later, she heard the front door open. Conan opened one eye and slapped his tail on the floor but didn't bother rising when Will came in carrying a small tool box and a container of nails.

He faltered a little when he saw her, as if he had forgotten her presence, or, worse, had maybe hoped it was all a bad dream. She was tempted again to abandon the whole idea and return upstairs to Maddie. But some part of her was still intensely curious to know why he seemed so uncomfortable in her presence.

He obviously wasn't completely impervious to her or he wouldn't care whether she hung around or not, any more than it bothered him to have Conan watching him work.

Was that a good sign, or just more evidence that she ought to just leave the poor man alone?

"Are you sure there's not anything else I can bring inside for you?" she asked. "I'm not good for much but I can carry tools or something."

"No. This should be everything I need."

He said nothing more, just started laying out tools, and she might have thought he had completely forgotten her presence if not for the barest clenching of muscle along his jawline and a hint of red at the tips of his ears.

She knew she shouldn't find that tiny reaction so fascinating but she couldn't seem to stop staring.

She found *everything* about Will Garrett fascinating, she acknowledged somewhat grimly.

From the tool belt riding low on his hips to the broad shoulders he had gained from hard work over the years to the tiny network of lines around his eyes that had probably once been laugh lines.

She wanted to hear him laugh again. The strength of her desire burned through her chest and she would have given anything just then to be able to come up with some kind of hilarious story that would be guaranteed to have him in stitches.

"Since you're here, can you do me a favor?" he spoke suddenly as she was wracking her brain trying to come up with something.

"Of course." She jumped up, pathetically grateful for any task, no matter how humble.

"I need to double check my measurements. I've checked them several times but I want to be sure before I make the final cuts."

"I guess you can't be too careful in your line of work."

"Not when you're dealing with oak trim that costs an arm and a leg," he answered.

"It's gorgeous, though."

"Worth every penny," he agreed, and for one breathless moment, he looked as if he wanted to smile. Just before the lighthearted expression would have broken free, his features sobered and he held out the end of the tape measure to her.

He was a man who devoted scrupulous attention to detail, she thought as they measured and re-measured the circumference of the room. He had kissed her the same way, thoroughly and completely, as if he couldn't bear the idea of missing a single second.

Her stomach quivered at the memory of his arms around her and the intensity of his mouth searching hers.

Maybe this hadn't been such a grand idea, the two

of them alone here in the quiet hush of a rainy day morning with only Conan for company.

"What do you do when you don't have a fumbling and inept—but well-meaning—assistant to help you out with things like this?" she asked, to break the sudden hushed intimacy.

He shrugged. "I usually make do. I have a couple of high school kids who help me sometimes. Most jobs I can handle on my own but sometimes an extra set of hands can definitely make the work a lot easier."

She was grateful again that she had offered help, even if he still seemed uneasy about accepting.

"Well, I can't promise that my hands are good for much, but I'm happy to use them for anything you need."

As soon as the words left her mouth, she realized how they could be misconstrued. She flushed, but to her vast relief he didn't seem to notice either her blush or her unintentionally provocative statement.

"Thanks. I appreciate that."

He paused after writing down one more measurement then retracting the tape measure. "Robin was always after me to hire a full-time assistant," he said after a moment.

This was the first time he had mentioned his wife to her on his own. It seemed an important step, somehow, as if he had allowed himself to lower yet another barrier between them.

Julia held her breath, not wanting to say anything that might make him regret bringing up the subject.

"You didn't do it, though?"

He shrugged. "I like working on my own. I can pick the music I want, can work at my own pace, can talk to myself when I need to. Yeah, I guess that probably makes me a little on the crazy side."

She laughed. "Not crazy. I talk to myself all the time. It helps to have Conan around, then I can at least pretend I'm talking to him."

He smiled. One moment he was wearing that remote, polite expression, then next, a genuine smile stole over his handsome features. She stared at it, her pulse shivering.

She wanted to leap up and down and shriek with glee that she had been able to lighten his features, even if only for a moment, but then he would definitely think *she* was the crazy one.

"Maybe I need a dog to take on jobs with me, just so I don't get a reputation as the wild-eyed carpenter who carries on long conversations with himself."

"I'm sure Sage and Anna would consider renting Conan out by the hour," she offered.

He smiled again—twice in as many minutes!—and turned to the dog. "What do you say, bud? Want to be my permanent assistant?"

Conan snuffled and gave a huge yawn that stretched his jaws, then he flopped over on his other side, turning his back toward both of them.

Julia couldn't help laughing. "Sorry, Will, but I think that's a definite no. You wouldn't want to interfere with his strenuous nap schedule. I guess you'll have to make do with me for now. I just hope I haven't messed up your rhythm too much."

"No. You're actually helping."

"You don't have to sound so surprised!" she exclaimed. "I do occasionally have my uses."

"Sorry. I didn't mean it that way."

She managed a smile. "No problem. Believe it or not, I've got a pretty thick skin."

They worked in silence and Will seemed deep in thought. When he spoke some time later, she realized his mind was still on what he'd said about hiring an assistant.

"Sometimes Robin would come with me on bigger jobs to lend a hand, until Cara came along, anyway," he said. "She started to crawl early—six months or so— and was into everything. She barely gave Robin a second to breathe for chasing her."

Again, she sensed by the stiff set of his shoulders that he wasn't completely comfortable talking about his family. She wasn't sure why he had decided to share these few details but she was beyond touched that he was willing to show her this snapshot of their life together.

"I can imagine it was hard to get any work done while you were chasing a busy toddler," she said.

He nodded. "She wasn't afraid of anything, our Cara. If Robin or I didn't watch her, she'd be out the back door and halfway to the ocean before we figured out where she had gone. We had to put double child-locks on every door."

He smiled a little at the memory but she could still sense the pain around the edges of his smile. She couldn't help herself, she reached out and touched his forearm, driven only by the need to comfort him.

His skin was warm, covered in a layer of crisp dark hair. He looked down at her fingers on his darker skin and she thought she saw his adam's apple move as he swallowed.

"Maddie was like that, too," she said after a moment, lifting her hand away.

"Maddie?"

"I know. Hard to believe. She was a much busier toddler than Simon. She was always the ringleader of the two of them."

She smiled at the memory. "When they still could barely walk, they used to climb out of their cribs in the night to play with their toys. I couldn't figure out how they were doing it so I set up the video camera with a motion sensor and caught Maddie moving like a little monkey to climb out of hers. She didn't need any help but Simon apparently wasn't as skilled so Maddie would climb out and then push a half-dozen stuffed animals over the top railing of his crib so he could use them to climb out. It was quite a system the little rascals came up with."

He paused in the middle of searching through his toolbox, his features far more interested than she might have expected. "So what did you do? Take out all the stuffed animals from the room?"

She made a face. "No. Gave into the inevitable. We bought them both toddler beds so they wouldn't break their necks climbing out"

"Did they still get up in the night?"

"Not as much. I think it was the lure of the forbidden that kept them trying to escape."

He laughed—a real, full-fledged laugh. She watched the shadows lift from his eyes for just a moment, saw in that light expression some glimmer of the Will she had known, and she could swear she felt the tumble and thud of her heart.

She was an idiot for Will Garrett, only now she didn't have the excuse of being fifteen, flush with the heady excitement of first love.

After entirely too short a time, his laughter slid away and he turned his attention back to the project. "How do you feel about heights?"

"Moderately okay, within reason."

"It would help if you could hold the trim up while I nail it, as long as you don't mind climbing the ladder."

"Not at all."

For the next twenty minutes, they spoke little as they worked together to hang the trim. They finished two walls quickly but the other two weren't as straightforward. One had a fireplace and chimney flue that Will needed to work the trim around and the other had a jog that she thought must contain ductwork.

As she waited for Will to figure out the angles for the

cuts, Julia sat on the couch, enjoying the animation on his features as he calculated. She wondered if he knew how his eyes lit up while he was working, how he seemed to vibrate with an energy she didn't see there at other times.

At last he figured out the math involved to make sure the moldings matched up correctly. He left for a moment and she heard his power saw out on the porch.

"You love this, don't you?" she asked when he returned carrying the cut pieces of trim.

He shrugged. "It's a living."

"It's more than that to you. I can tell. I keep remembering how much you complained about your dad making you go out on jobs with him that summer."

His laugh was rueful, tinged with embarrassment. "I was a stupid sixteen-year-old punk without a brain in my head. All I wanted to do was hang out with my friends and try to impress pretty girls."

She shook her head. "You were *not* a punk. You were by far the most decent boy I knew."

The tips of his ears turned that dusky red again. "Funny, you always seemed like such a sensible kind of girl."

"I was sensible enough to know when a boy is different from the others I'd met. All they wanted to do was flirt and see how many bases they could steal. They weren't interested in talking about serious things like the political science class they had taken the year before or the ecological condition of the shoreline."

"Did I do that?"

"You don't remember?"

He slanted her a sidelong look. "All I remember is trying to figure out whether I dared try sliding into second base."

She blushed, though she couldn't help smiling, too. "I guess you were just more subtle about that particular goal than the other boys, then."

"Either that or more chicken."

She laughed. She couldn't help herself. To her delight, he laughed along with her and the unexpected sound of it even had Conan lifting his head to watch the two of them with what looked suspiciously like satisfaction.

She remembered Sage's assertion that the dog was working in cahoots with Abigail.

Just now—with the rain pattering softly against the window and this peculiar intimacy swirling around them—the idea didn't seem completely ludicrous.

"Okay, I think I've finally got this figured out," he said after a moment. "I think I'm ready for my assistant."

She pushed her ladder closer to his since they were working with a much smaller length of trim.

As he was only a few feet away from her, she was intensely aware of him—his scent, leathery and masculine, and the heat that seemed to pulse from him.

He wasn't smiling or laughing now, she noted. In fact, he seemed tense suddenly and in a hurry to finish this section of the job.

"I can probably handle the rest on my own," he said, his voice suddenly sounding strained. "None of the remaining lengths of trim are very long so I shouldn't need your help holding them in place."

"I can stick around, just in case you need me."

His gaze met hers and she thought he would tell her not to bother but he simply nodded. "Sure. Okay."

She was so relieved he wasn't going to send her away that she wasn't paying as close attention to what she was doing as she should have been while she descended the ladder at the same time Will descended his own ladder next to her.

In her distracted state, she misjudged the last rung and stumbled a little at the bottom.

"Whoa! Careful there," he exclaimed, reaching out instinctively to catch her.

For one moment, they froze in that suspended state, with his strong arms around her and her arms trapped between their bodies. Her startled gaze flew to his and she thought she saw awareness and desire and the barest shadow of resignation there.

Will stared at her, his heart pumping in his chest like an out-of-control nail gun. A desperate kind of hunger prowled through him, wild and urgent. Though he knew she was far from it, she felt small and fragile in his arms.

He could feel the heat of her burning his skin, could smell that soft, mouthwatering scent of cherry blossoms.

He closed his eyes, fighting the inevitable with every ounce of strength he had left. But when he opened his eyes, he found her color high, her lips parted slightly, her eyes a deep and mossy green, shadowed with what he was almost positive was a heady awareness to match his own.

He should stop this right now, should just release her, push her from Anna's apartment and lock the door snugly behind her. The tiny corner of his brain that could still manage to string together a coherent thought told him that was exactly the course of action he ought to follow.

But how could he? She was so soft, so sweetly, irresistibly warm, and he had been cold for so damn long.

He heard a groan and realized it came from his own throat just an instant before he lowered his mouth and kissed her.

She sighed his name, just a whispered breath between their mouths, but the sound seemed to sink through all the layers of careful protection around his heart.

She wrapped her arms around his neck, responding eagerly to his kiss. Tenderness surged through him, raw and terrifying. He wanted to hang on tight and never let go, wanted to stand in Abigail's old living room for the rest of his life with a soft rain clicking against the windows and Julia Hudson Blair in his arms.

They kissed for a long time, until he was breathing hard and light-headed, until her mouth was swollen, until his body cried out for more and more.

He didn't know how long they would have continued—forever if he'd had his way—when suddenly he heard the one thing guaranteed to shatter the moment and the mood like a hard, cold downpour.

"Mama? Are you there? I woke up."

The sweet, high voice cut through the room like a buzz saw. He stiffened, his insides cold suddenly, and frantically looked to the doorway, aghast at what he had done and that her daughter had caught them at it.

He only knew a small measure of relief when he realized the voice was coming from the walkie-talkie she had brought downstairs.

Julia was breathing just as hard as he was, her eyes wide and dazed and her cheeks flushed.

Even through his dismay, he had to clench his fists at his side to keep from reaching for her again.

She drew in a deep, shuddering breath, then walked to the walkie-talkie and picked it up.

"I'm here, baby," she said, her voice slightly ragged. "How are you feeling?"

"My throat still hurts a little but I'm okay," Maddie answered. "Where are you, Mama?"

Julia flashed a quick glance at him, then looked away. "Downstairs with W— Mr. Garrett. Didn't you see my note?"

"Yes, when I woke up. But I was just wondering if you were still down there."

"I am."

"Is Conan there with you?"

Will saw her sweep the room with her gaze until she found the dog still curled up by the couch. "He's right here. I'll bring him up with me if you want some company."

"Thanks, Mama."

She clipped the walkie-talkie to her belt, angled slightly away from him so he couldn't see her expression, then she seemed to draw another deep breath before she turned to face him.

"I...have to go up. Maddie needs me."

"Right." He ached to touch her again, just one more time, but he fiercely clamped down on the desire, wanting her gone almost as much as he wanted to sweep her into his arms again.

Without warning, he was suddenly furious. Damn her, *damn her*, for making him want again—for this churn of his blood pouring into the frozen edges inside him. Pain prickled through him, like he had just shoved frostbitten fingers into boiling water.

He didn't want this, didn't want to feel again. Hadn't he made that clear? So why the hell did she have to come in here, with her sweet smile and her warm eyes and her soft curves.

"Will—"

"Don't say anything," he bit out. "This was a mistake. It's been a mistake for me to spend even a minute with you since you came back to town."

At his sudden attack, shock and hurt flared in her

green eyes and he hated himself all over again but that didn't change what he knew he had to do.

"You didn't think it was a mistake a moment ago," she murmured.

He couldn't deny the truth of that. "I'm attracted to you. That's obvious, isn't it? I have been since I was sixteen years old. But I don't want to be. You're in my way every single time I turn around."

He lashed out, needing only to make her understand even as he was appalled at his words, at the way her spine seemed to stiffen with each syllable.

Still, he couldn't seem to hold them back once he started. They gushed between them, ugly and harsh.

"You're always coming around to help me work, showing up at my house dragging your kids along, crowding me every second. Don't you get it? I don't want you around! Why can't you just leave me alone?"

Conan rose and growled and for the first time in Will's memory the dog looked menacing. At the same time, a branch outside Anna's apartment clawed and scratched against the window, whipped by a sudden microburst of wind.

Julia seemed to ignore all the external distractions. She drew in a deep breath, her face paler than he had ever seen it.

"That's not fair," she said, her voice low and tight.

He raked a hand through his hair, hating himself, hating her, hating Robin and Cara for leaving him this empty, harsh, cruel husk of a man. "I know. I know it's not fair. You don't deserve to bear the weight of all that, Julia. I know that, but I can't help it. I'm sorry, but it's the truth. I need you to leave me alone. Please. I can't do this anymore. I can't. Not with you. Not with anyone."

The branch scraped the glass harder and he made a mental note to prune it for Sage and Anna, even as he fought down the urge to pound something, to smash his fists hard into the new drywall he had put in a few months earlier.

She studied him for a long moment, her features taut.

"Okay," she finally murmured and headed for the door to Anna's apartment.

Before she left, she turned around to face him one last time. "I appreciate your frankness. Since I know you're a fair man, I'm sure you'll allow me the same privilege."

What the hell was he supposed to say to that? He waited, though he wanted nothing more than to shove the door closed behind her and lock it tight.

"I have something I want to say, though I know it's not my place and none of my business. Still, I think you need to hear it from someone."

She paused, and seemed to be gathering her thoughts. When she spoke, her words sliced at him like a band saw.

"Will, do you really think Robin and Cara would want this for you?"

"Don't."

He couldn't bear a lecture or a commentary or whatever she planned. Not now, not about this.

She shook her head. "No. I'm going to say this. And then you can push me away all you want, as you've been doing since I came back to Cannon Beach. I want you to ask yourself if your wife and little girl would want you to spend the rest of your life wallowing in your pain, smothering yourself in it. From all I've heard about Robin, it sounds as if she was generous and loving to everyone. Sage has told me what a good friend she was to everyone, how people were always drawn to her because of her kindness and her cheerful nature. I'm sorry I never had the chance to meet her. But from what I've heard of her, I can't imagine Robin would find it any tribute to her kind and giving nature that you want you to close yourself away from life as some kind of…of penance because she's gone."

She looked as if she had more she wanted to say, but to his relief she only gave him one more long look then turned to gesture to Conan. The dog added his glare to hers, giving Will what could only be described as the snake-eye, then followed her out the door.

Will stood for a long moment, an ache in his chest and her scent still swirling around him. He closed his eyes, remembering again the sweetness of her touch, how fiercely he had wanted to hold on tight, to surrender completely and let her work her healing magic.

He had to leave.

That was all there was to it. He couldn't stay in Cannon Beach with Julia and her kids just a few houses away. There was no way in the small community of year-round residents that he could avoid her, and seeing her, spending any time with her, was obviously a mistake.

He had meant what he said. She crowded him and he couldn't deal with it anymore.

He knew after his outburst just now that she wouldn't make any effort to spend time with him, but they were still bound to bump into each other once in a while and he had just proved to himself that he had no powers of resistance where she was concerned.

He had no other option but to escape.

He pulled out his cell phone. He knew the number was there—he had dialed it only the night before but in the end he had lost his nerve and hung up.

With the wind still whipping the tree branches outside like angry fists, he found it quickly, hit the button to redial and waited for it to ring.

As he might have expected, he was sent immediately to voice-messaging. For a moment he considered hanging up again but the sweet scent of spring flowers drifted to him and he knew this was what he had to do.

He drew in a breath. "Eben, this is Will Garrett," he began. "I'd like to talk about your offer, if it's still open."

Chapter Twelve

"Simon, hands to yourself."

Her son snatched his fingers back an instant before they would have dipped into the frosting on the frill-bedecked sheet cake for Sage's wedding shower.

"I only wanted a little smackeral," he complained.

Julia sighed, even as she fought a smile. This was why she was destined to be a lousy mother, she decided. How on earth was she supposed to have the gumption to properly discipline her son when he knew he could charm her every time by quoting Winnie the Pooh?

"No smackerals, little or otherwise," she said as sternly as she could manage. "After the bridal shower you can have all the leftovers you want but Sage wouldn't want grimy little finger trails dipping through her pretty cake, would she?"

"Sage wouldn't mind," he grumbled.

All right, he was probably correct on that observation. Sage was remarkably even-tempered for a bride and she adored Julia's twins and spoiled them both relentlessly.

But as their mother, it was Julia's responsibility to teach them little things like manners, and she couldn't let him get away with it, smackerals or not.

"I mind," she said firmly. "Tell you what, if you promise to help Anna and me put all the chairs and tables away after the shower, you can appease your sugar buzz with one of the cookies you and Maddie and I made last night."

He grinned and reached for one. "Can I take one to Mad? She's in her room."

"As long as you don't forget where you were taking it and eat that one too along the way."

"I would *never* do that!" he protested, with just a shade too much offended innocence.

Julia shook her head, smiling as she put the finishing touches on the cake.

Simon paused at the doorway. "Can we eat our cookies outside and play with Conan for awhile since the rain *finally* stopped?"

"Of course," she answered. After an entire week straight of rain, she knew both of her children were suffering from acute cases of cabin fever.

A moment later, she heard the door slam then the

pounding of two little sets of feet hurtling down the stairs, joined shortly after by enthusiastic barking.

Unable to resist, she moved to the window overlooking the backyard just in time to see Maddie pick up an armful of fallen leaves and toss them into the air, her face beaming with joy at being outside to savor the October sunshine. Not far away, Conan and Simon were already wrestling in the grass together.

The two of them loved this place—the old house, with its quirks and its personality, the yard and Abigail's beautiful gardens, the wild and gorgeous ocean just a few footsteps away.

They were thriving here, just as she had hoped. They already had good friends at school, they were doing well in their classes. Maddie's health seemed to have taken a giant leap forward and improved immeasurably in the nearly two months they had been in Cannon Beach.

She should be so happy. Her children were happy, her job was working out well, they had all settled into a routine.

So why couldn't she shake this lingering depression that seemed to have settled on her shoulders as summer slid into autumn? She shifted her gaze from the Brambleberry House yard to another house just a few hundred yards up the beach.

There was the answer to the question of why she couldn't seem to shake her gray mood. Will Garrett. She hadn't seen him since their disastrous encounter nearly two weeks earlier but her insides still churned with dismay when she remembered his blunt words telling her to leave him alone, and then her own presumptuous reply.

She had been way out of line to bring Robin and Cara into the whole thing, to basically accuse him of dishonoring his wife and daughter's memory simply because he continued to push Julia away.

She had had no right to tell him how he ought to grieve or to pretend she knew what his wife might have wanted for him. She had never even met the woman.

Because of her lingering shame at her own temerity, she was almost grateful she hadn't seen him since, even to catch a glimpse of him through the pines as he moved around his house.

That's what she told herself, anyway. If she stood at her window at night watching the lights in his house, hoping for some shadow to move across a window, well, that was her own pathetic little secret.

With one last sigh, she forced herself to move away from the window and return to the kitchen and the cake. A few moments later, with a final flourish, she judged it ready and carefully picked it up to carry it downstairs to Anna's apartment.

Since her arms were full, she managed to ring the doorbell with her elbow. Anna opened almost immediately. Though she smiled, Julia didn't miss the troubled expression in her eyes.

She was probably just busy setting up for the shower, Julia told herself. She knew Anna had been distracted with problems at her two giftshops as well, though she seemed reluctant to talk about them.

Julia smiled and held out the cake. "Watch out. Masterpiece coming through."

Anna's expression lifted slightly as she looked at the autumn-themed cake, with its richly colored oak and maple leaves and pine boughs, all crafted of frosting.

Sage wasn't one for frilly lace and other traditional wedding decorations. Given her job as a naturalist and her love of the outdoors, Julia and Anna had picked a nature theme for the shower they were throwing and the cake was to be the centerpiece of their decorations.

"Oh! Oh, It's beautiful!"

"Told you it would be," Julia said with undeniable satisfaction as she carried the cake inside Anna's apartment to a table set in a corner.

"You were absolutely right," Sage said from the couch. "I can't believe you did all that in one afternoon!"

Julia shrugged. "I don't have a lot of domestic skills but I can decorate a cake like nobody's business. I told you I put myself through college working in a bakery, so if the teaching thing ever falls through, I've at least got something to fall back on."

She grinned at them both and was surprised when they didn't smile back. Instead, they exchanged grim looks.

"What is it? What's wrong? Is it the cake? I tried to decorate it just as we discussed."

"It's not the cake," Anna assured her. "The cake is gorgeous."

"Did somebody cancel, then?"

"No. Everybody's still coming, as far as I know." Sage sighed. "I just hung up the phone with Eben."

She frowned. "Is everything okay with Chloe?"

"No. Nothing like that. Julia, it's not Eben or Chloe or anything to do with the shower. It's Will."

Her stomach cramped suddenly and for a moment she couldn't seem to breathe. "What...what's wrong with Will?"

"He's leaving," Anna said, her usual matter-of-fact tone sounding strained.

"Leaving?"

Sage nodded, her eyes distressed. "Apparently he's taken a traveling job with Spencer Hotels. A sort of carpentry trouble-shooter, traveling around to their renovation sites and overseeing the work of the local builders. He's starting right after the wedding. He accepted the job a few weeks ago but apparently Eben didn't seem to think it was anything worth mentioning to me until just now on the phone, purely in passing."

She scowled, apparently at her absent fiancé. Julia barely noticed, too lost in her own shock. Two weeks ago. She didn't miss the significance of that, not for a minute.

They had kissed right here in this very living room

and she could think of nothing else but how he had all but begged her to leave him alone and then in her hurt, she had said such nervy, terrible things to him.

Ask yourself if your wife and little girl would want you to spend the rest of your life wallowing in your pain, smothering yourself in it.

Oh, what had she done? Now he had taken a traveling job with Eben's company and she could hardly seem to work her brain around it. He was leaving Cannon Beach—the home he loved, his friends, the business he had work so hard to build.

Because of her.

She knew it had to be so. What other reason could he have?

She had made him too uncomfortable, had pushed too hard.

I can't imagine Robin would find it any tribute that you want you to close yourself away from life as some kind of penance because she's gone.

Her face burned and her stomach seemed to twist into a snarled tangle. What had she *done?*

"What do you think, Julia?"

She jerked her mind back to the conversation to realize Sage was speaking to her and as her silence dragged on, both women were giving her curious looks.

It was obvious they expected some response from her but as she hadn't heard the question, she didn't know at all what to say.

"I'm sorry. What?"

"I said that you've known him longer than any of us. What could he be thinking?"

"Oh no. I don't know him," she murmured. "Not really."

Perhaps that was the trouble, she admitted to herself. She had this idealized image of Will from years ago when she had loved him as a girl. Had she truly allowed herself to accept the reality of all the years and the pain between them?

She had pushed him, harder than he was ready to be pushed. She had backed him into a corner and he was looking for some way out.

This was all her fault and she was going to have to figure out a way to make things right. She couldn't let Will leave everything he cared about behind because of her.

The doorbell rang suddenly and Conan jumped up from his spot on the floor where he had been watching them. Now he hurried to Anna's open apartment door, his tail wagging furiously and for one wild moment her heart jumped at the thought that it might be Will.

Foolish, she realized almost instantly. Why would he be here?

More likely it was Becca Wilder, the teenager she had hired to corral the twins for the evening while she was busy with Sage's shower.

Her supposition was confirmed a moment later when Anna went to answer the door and Julia heard the voice of Jewel Wilder, Becca's mother and one of Sage's friends, who had offered to drop Becca off when she came to the shower herself.

She couldn't do anything about Will right now, she realized. Sage's bridal shower was supposed to start any moment now and she couldn't let the celebration be ruined by her guilt.

Three hours later, as Sage said good-bye to the last of her guests, Julia began gathering discarded plates and cups, doing her best to ignore her head that throbbed and pulsed with pain.

She knew exactly why her head was pounding—the same reason her heart ached. Because of Will and his stubborn determination to shut himself off from life and because of her own stubborn, misguided determination to prevent him.

For Sage's sake, she had done her best to put away her anxiety and guilt for the evening. She had laughed and played silly wedding shower games and tried to enjoy watching Sage open the gifts from her eclectic collection of friends.

Beneath it all, the ache simmered and seethed, like a vat of bitter bile waiting to boil over.

Will was leaving his home, his friends, his wife and daughter's resting places. She couldn't let him do it, not if he was leaving because of her.

She carried the plates and dishes into the kitchen, where she found Anna wrapping up the leftover food.

"It was a wonderful party," Julia said.

"I think everyone had a good time," Anna agreed. "But listen, you don't have to help clean up. I can handle it. Why don't you go on upstairs with the twins?"

"I just checked with Becca and they're both down for the night. She's heading home with her mom and is leaving the door open so we can hear them down here."

Anna stuck a plate of little sandwiches into her refrigerator, then gave Julia a placid smile.

"That's great. Since the twins are asleep, this would be the perfect chance for you to go and talk some sense into Will."

Julia stared at her, completely astounded at the suggestion. "Where did that come from?"

Anna smiled. "My brilliantly insightful mind."

"Which I never realized until this moment is a little on the cracked side. Why would he listen to me?"

"Well, somebody needs to knock some sense into him and Sage and I both decided you're the best one for the job."

"Why on earth would you possibly think *that?* You've both been friends with him for a long time. I just moved back. He'll listen to what you have to say long before he'll listen to me."

Not to mention the tiny little detail that she suspected *she* was the reason he was leaving in the first place— and the fact that he had basically ordered her to stay away from him.

She wasn't about to admit that to Anna, though.

"We're like sisters to him," Anna answered. "Naggy, annoying little sisters. You, on the other hand, are the woman he has feelings for."

She bobbled the plate she was loading into the dishwasher but managed to catch it before it shattered on the floor.

"Wrong!" she exclaimed. "Oh, you couldn't be more wrong. Will doesn't have feelings for me. He…he might, if he would let himself, but he's wrapped himself up so tightly in his pain he won't let anyone through. Or not me, at least. No, he absolutely doesn't have feelings for me."

Anna studied her for a long moment, then smiled unexpectedly. "Our mistake, then, I guess. Sage and I were quite convinced there was something between the two of you. Will's been different ever since you came back to Cannon Beach."

"Different, how?" she asked warily.

"I can't quite put my finger on how, exactly. I wouldn't say he's been happier, but he's done things he hasn't in two years. Going for ice cream with you and your kids. Coming to the barbecue with Eben and Chloe without putting up a fight. Sage and I both thought you were slowly dragging him back to life, whether he wanted you to or not, and we were both thrilled about it. He kissed you, didn't he?"

Julia flushed. "Yes, but he wasn't happy about either time."

Anna's eyebrow rose. "There was more than one time?"

She sighed. "A few weeks ago, when I helped him hang the new moldings in your living room. We had a fight afterward and I said horrible things to him, things I had no right to say. And now I find out he took a job with Eben's company, and accepted it two weeks ago. I just can't believe it's a coincidence."

"All the more reason you should be the one to convince him to stay," Anna said.

"He told me to stay away from him," Julia whispered, hurting all over again at the harshness of his words.

"Are you going to listen to him? Go on," Anna urged. "I'll keep an eye on Simon and Maddie for you. There's nothing stopping you."

Except maybe her guilt and her nerves and the horrible, sinking sensation in her gut that she was pushing a man away from everything that he cared about, just so he could escape from her.

Before she could formulate further arguments, a huge shaggy beast suddenly hurried into the room, a leash in his mouth and Sage right on his heels.

"Conan, what has gotten into you, you crazy dog?" she exclaimed. "I can put you out."

But the dog didn't listen to her. He headed straight to Julia, plopped down at her feet and held the leash out in his mouth with that familiar expectant look.

She groaned. "Not you, too?"

Sage and Anna exchanged glances and Julia was quite certain she heard Sage snigger.

"Looks like you're the chosen one," Anna said with a smile.

"You can't fight your destiny, Jules," Sage piped in. "Believe me, I've tried. The King of Brambleberry House has declared you're tonight's sacrificial lamb. You can't escape your fate."

She closed her eyes, aware as she did that the pain in her head seemed to have lifted while she was talking to Anna. "I suppose you're telling me Conan wants me to talk to Will, too."

"That's what it looks like to me," Sage said.

"Same here."

Julia stared at Anna—prosaic, no-nonsense Anna, who looked just as convinced as Sage.

"You're both crazy. He's a dog, for heaven's sake!"

Sage grinned. "Watch it. If you offend him, you'll be stuck for life giving him his evening walk."

"Rain or shine," Anna added. "And around here, it's usually rain."

She studied them all looking so expectantly at her and gave a sigh of resignation. "This isn't fair, you know. The three of you ganging up on me like this."

In answer, Sage clipped the leash on Conan's collar and held the end out for Julia. Anna left the room, returning a moment later with Julia's jacket from the closet in the entryway.

"What if Will doesn't want to talk to me?"

It was a purely rhetorical question. She knew perfectly well he wouldn't want to talk to her, just as she was grimly aware she was only trying to delay the inevitable moment when she had to gather her nerve and walk down the beach to his house.

"You're an elementary school teacher," Anna said with a confident grin. "You're good at making your students do things they don't want to do, aren't you?"

Julia snorted. "I have a feeling Will Garrett might be just a tad harder to manage than my fifth-grade boys."

"We all have complete faith in you," Sage said.

Before she was quite aware of how they had managed it, they ushered her and Conan out the front door and closed it behind her. She was quite surprised when she didn't hear the click of the door locking behind her. She wouldn't have put anything past them at this point.

Conan strained on his leash to be gone but she stood on the porch steps of Brambleberry House trying to gather her frayed nerves as she listened to the distant crash of the sea and the cool October breeze moaning in the tops of the pines.

Finally she couldn't ignore Conan's urgency and she followed the walkway around the house to the gate that opened to the beach.

It would probably be a quicker route to just take the road to his house but she wasn't in a huge hurry to face him anyway.

Conan seemed less insistent as they walked along the shoreline, after he had marked just about every single rock and tuft of grass they passed.

It gave her time to remember her last summer on Cannon Beach. She passed the rock where she had been sitting when he kissed her for the *last* time—not counting more recent incidences—the night before she left Cannon Beach when she was fifteen.

She paused and ran her finger along the uneven surface, remembering the thrill of his arms around her and how she had been so very certain she had to be in love with him.

She'd had nothing to compare it to, but she had been quite sure at fifteen that this must be the real thing.

And then the next day her world had shattered and she had been shuttled to Sacramento with her mother, away from everything safe and secure in her life.

Still, even as her parents' marriage had imploded, she had held the memory of a handsome boy close to her heart.

At first she thought the moisture on her cheeks was just sea spray, then she realized it was tears, that she was crying for lost innocence and for the two people they had been, and for all the pain that had come after for both of them.

She wiped at her cheeks as she knelt and hugged Conan to her. The dog licked at her cheeks and she smiled a little at his attempts to comfort her.

"I'm being silly again, aren't I? I'm not fifteen anymore and I'm not that dreamy-eyed girl. I'm thirty-one years old and I need to start acting like it, don't I?"

The dog barked as if he agreed with her.

With renewed resolve, she squared her shoulders and stood again, gathering her courage around her.

She had to do this. Will's life was here in Cannon Beach. It had always been here, and she couldn't ruin that for him.

She swallowed her nerves and headed for the lights she could see flickering in his workshop.

Chapter Thirteen

He would miss this.

Will stood in his father's workshop—his workspace now, at least for another few days—and routered the edge of a shingle while a blues station played on the stereo.

He had always found comfort within these walls, with the air sweet with freshly cut wood shavings and sawdust motes drifting in the air, catching the light like gold flakes.

He left the door ajar, both for ventilation and to let the cool, moist sea air inside. In the quiet intervals without the whine and hum of his power tools, he could hear the ocean's low murmur just down the beach.

This was his favorite spot in the world, the place where he had learned his craft, where he had forged a connection with his stern, sometimes austere father, where he had figured out many of his own strengths and his weaknesses.

Before Robin and Cara died, he used to come out here so he could have a quiet place to think. Sage probably would have given it some hippy new age name like a transcendental meditation room or something.

He just always considered it the one place where his thoughts seemed more clear and cohesive.

He didn't so much need a place to think these days as he needed an escape on the nights when the house seemed too full of ghosts to hold anyone still breathing.

In a few days when he started working for Eben Spencer's company, everything would be different. He expected his workspaces for the next few months would be any spare corner he could find in whatever hotel around the globe where Eben sent him to work.

Who would have ever expected him to become an itinerant carpenter? *Have tools, will travel.*

His first job was outside of Boston but Eben wanted to send him to Madrid next and then on to Portofino, Italy before he headed to the Pacific Rim. And that was only the first month.

Will shook his head. Italy and Spain and Singapore. What the hell was he going to do in a foreign country where he didn't know a soul and didn't speak the language?

It all seemed wildly exotic for a guy who rarely left

his coastal hometown, who only possessed a current passport because he and Robin had gone on a cruise to Mexico the year before Cara came along.

The work would be the same. That was the important thing. He would still be doing the one thing he was good at, the one thing that filled him with satisfaction, whether he was in Portofino or Madrid or wherever else Eben sent him.

Maybe those ghosts might even have a chance to rest if he wasn't here dredging them up every minute.

He sure hoped he was making the right choice.

He set down the finished shingle and picked up another one from the dwindling pile next to him. Only a few more and then he only had to nail them to the roof to be finished. A few more hours of work ought to do it.

Against his will, he shot another glance out the window at the big house on the hill, solid and graceful against the moonlit sky.

The lights were out on the second floor, he noted immediately, then chided himself for even noticing.

He was almost certain he wasn't really trying to outrun any ghosts by taking the job with Spencer Hotels. But he knew he couldn't say the same for the living woman who haunted him.

He sighed as his thoughts inevitably slid back to Julia, as they had done so often the last two weeks. Tonight was Sage's bridal shower, he knew. He had seen cars coming and going all night.

Julia was probably right in the middle of it all, with her sweet smile and the sunshine she seemed to carry with her into every room.

For a man who wanted to push her away, he sure spent a hell of a lot of time thinking about her. He sighed again, and could almost swear he smelled the cherry blossom scent of her on the wind.

But a moment later, when the router was silent as he picked up another shingle, he thought he heard a snuffling kind of noise outside the door, then a dark red nose poked through.

An instant later, Conan was barking a greeting at him and Julia was walking through the doorway behind him.

Will yanked up his safety glasses and could do nothing but stare at her, wondering how his thoughts had possibly conjured her up.

Her cheeks were flushed, her hair tousled a little by the wind, but she was definitely flesh and blood.

"Hi," she murmured, and he was certain her color climbed a little higher on her cheeks.

She looked fragile and lovely and highly uncomfortable. No wonder, after the things he had said to her the last time they had spoken.

"I'm sorry to bother you… I… we…" Her voice trailed off.

"Wasn't tonight Sage's big bridal shower?"

"It was. But it's over now and everyone's gone. After the shower, Conan needed a walk and he picked me to take him and Sage and Anna made me come down here to talk to you."

She finished in a rush, without meeting his gaze.

"They made you?"

Her gaze finally flashed to his and he saw a combination of chagrin and rueful acceptance. "You know what they're like. I have a tough enough time saying no to them individually. When they combine forces, I'm pretty much helpless to resist."

"Why did they want you to talk to me?" he asked, though he had a pretty strong inkling.

She didn't answer him, though, only moved past him into the workshop, her attention suddenly caught by the project he was working on.

Damn it.

He could feel his own cheeks start to flush and wished, more than anything, that he had had the foresight to grab a tarp to cover the thing the minute she walked in.

"Will," she exclaimed. "It's gorgeous!"

He scratched the back of his neck, doing his best to ignore how the breathy excitement in her voice sent a shiver rippling down his spine. "It's not finished. I'm working on the shingles tonight, then I should be ready to take it back up to Brambleberry House."

She moved forward for a closer look and he couldn't seem to wrench his gaze away from her starry-eyed delight at the repaired dollhouse he had agreed to work on the day she moved in.

"It's absolutely stunning!"

She drew her finger along the curve of one of the cupola's with tender care. Will could only watch, grimly aware that he shouldn't have such an instant reaction just from the sight of her soft, delicate hands on his work.

"You fixed it! No, you didn't just fix it. This is beyond a simple repair. It was such a mess, just a pile of broken sticks, when you started! And from that, you've created a work of art!"

"I don't know that I'd go quite that far."

"I would! Oh, Will, it's beautiful. Better than it ever was, even when it was new from my father."

To his horror, tears started to well up in her eyes.

"It's just a dollhouse. Not worth bawling about," he said tersely, trying to keep the sudden panic out of his voice.

She gave a short laugh as she swiped at her cheeks. "They're happy tears. Oh, believe me. Will, it's wonderful. I can't tell you how much this will mean to Maddie. She tried to be brave about it but she was so heartbroken when I told her the dollhouse hadn't survived the move. It was one of her last few ties to her father and she has always cherished it, I think because he gave it to her right after her diagnosis, a few days before he…"

Her voice trailed off for a moment and he thought she wasn't going to complete the sentence, but then she drew in a breath and straightened her shoulders. "Before he left us."

Will stared at her, trying to make sense of her words.

"I didn't realize your husband died so soon after Maddie's cancer was discovered."

She sighed. "He didn't," she said slowly. "His car accident was eighteen months after her diagnosis but... we were separated most of that time. We were a few months shy of finalizing our divorce when he died."

She lifted her chin almost defiantly when she spoke the last part of the sentence.

He wondered at it, even as he tried to figure out how the hell a man with a beautiful wife and two kids—one with cancer—could walk away from his family in the middle of a crisis.

He left us, she had said quite plainly. He didn't miss the meaning of that now. The man had a daughter with cancer and he had been the one to walk away from them.

Will had a sudden fierce wish that he could have met her husband just once before he died, to teach the bastard a lesson about what it meant to be a man.

She was waiting for him to answer, he realized.

"I'm sorry," he finally said, wincing at the inane words. "That must have been hard on you and the kids during such a rough time."

She managed a wobbly smile. "You could say that."

"All this time, you never said anything about your marriage. I had no idea it was rocky."

She sighed and leaned against the work table holding the resurrected dollhouse.

"I don't talk about it much, especially when the kids

are around. I don't want them thinking less of their father."

He raised an eyebrow at that, but said nothing. He had his own opinions about it but he didn't think she would be eager to hear them.

"Maddie's diagnosis kicked Kevin in the gut. The stark truth is, he just couldn't handle it. His mother died of cancer when he was young, a particularly vicious form that lingered for a long time, and I think he just couldn't bear the thought that he might lose someone else he loved in the same way."

What kind of strength had it taken her to deal with a crumbling marriage at the same time she was fighting for her daughter's life? He couldn't even imagine it.

He studied her there in his workshop and saw shadows in her eyes. There was more to the story, he sensed.

"Was there someone else?" Some instinct prompted him to ask.

She gave him a swift, shocked look. "How did you know that? I haven't told anyone else. Not even Sage and Anna know that part."

"I don't know. Just a guess." He couldn't very well tell her he was becoming better than he ought to be at reading her thoughts in her lovely green eyes.

She sighed, tracing a finger over one of the arched windows on the dollhouse. "A coworker. He swore he only turned to her after we separated—after Maddy's diagnosis—because he was hurting so much inside and so afraid for the future."

"That doesn't take away much of the sting for you, I imagine."

"No. No, it doesn't. I was angry and bitter for a long time. I mean, I was the one dealing with appointments and sitting through Maddie's chemotherapy with her and holding her when she threw up for hours afterward. I was scared, too. Not scared, I was *terrified*. I used to check on her dozens of times a night, just to make sure she was still breathing. I still do when she's having a rough night. It was a miracle I could function, most days. I was just as scared, but I didn't turn to someone else. I toughed it out by myself because I had no choice."

He couldn't imagine such a betrayal—more than that, he couldn't understand why she could seem to be such a happy person now after what she had been through.

Most women he knew would be bitter and angry at the world after surviving such an ordeal but Julia seemed to bubble over with joy, finding delight in everything.

She had been over the moon that he had repaired a dollhouse her bastard of an almost-ex-husband had worked on. He figured most betrayed women would have smashed the dollhouse to pieces themselves out of spite so they wouldn't have one more reminder of their cheating spouse.

"I don't know why I told you all that," she said after a moment, her cheeks slightly pink. "I didn't come here to relive the past."

Since she seemed eager to change the subject, he decided he wouldn't push her.

"That's right," he answered. "Sage and Anna sent you."

"I would have come anyway," she admitted. "They just gave me a push in this direction."

He found that slightly hard to believe, given his rudeness the last time they met.

"Why?" he asked.

She let out a breath, then confirmed his suspicion. "I…Sage just found out from Eben tonight that you're leaving."

He picked up another shingle, stalling for time. He did *not* want to get into this, especially not with her, though he had been half-expecting something like this for two weeks, since he accepted Eben's offer.

"That's right," he finally said. It would have been rude to turn the router on again—not to mention, Conan wouldn't like it—but he was severely tempted, if only to cut her off.

She seemed to have become inordinately fascinated with one of the finials on the dollhouse.

"I know this is presumptuous and I have no real right to ask…"

Her voice trailed off and he sighed, yanking his safety glasses off his head and setting them aside. He had a feeling he wasn't going to be finishing the doll-house anytime soon.

"Something tells me you're going to ask anyway."

She twisted her hands together, her color still high. "You love Cannon Beach, Will. I know you do."

"Yeah. I do love it here. I always have."

"Help me understand, then, why you would suddenly decide to leave the town you have lived in for thirty-two years. This is your home. You have friends here, a thriving business. Your whole life is here!"

"What life?"

He hadn't meant to say something that raw, that honest, but his words seemed to hang between them and he couldn't yank them back.

It was the truth, anyway.

He didn't have a life, or at least not much of one. Everything he had known and cared about was gone and he couldn't walk anywhere in Cannon Beach without stumbling over a memory of a time when he thought he had owned the world, when he was certain he had everything he could ever possibly want.

Since Julia came to town, everything seemed so much harder, his world so much emptier—something else he wasn't about to explain to her.

Her eyes were dark with sorrow and something else that looked suspiciously like guilt.

"Maybe I was ready for a change," he finally said. "You just said it yourself, I've lived here my entire life. That's pretty pathetic for a grown man to admit, that he's never been anywhere, never done anything. Eben offered me the job some time ago. I gave it a lot of thought and finally decided the time was right."

She didn't look convinced. After another long, awkward moment, she clenched her hands together and lifted her gaze to his, her mouth trembling slightly.

"Will you tell me the truth? Are you leaving because of me?"

He shifted his gaze away, wishing his hands were busy with the router again. Unfortunately, his gaze collided with Conan's, and the dog gave him an entirely too perceptive look.

"Why would you say that?" he stalled.

She stepped closer, looking again as if she wanted to weep. "I've been sick inside ever since Sage told me you were taking this job with Eben's company."

"You shouldn't be, Julia. This is not on you. Let it go."

She shook her head. "I pushed you too hard the other day. I said terrible things. I had no right, Will. I have a terrible habit of always thinking I know what's best for everyone else."

Her short laugh held no trace of humor. "I don't know why. I mean, I've made a complete mess of my own life, haven't I? So why would I dare think I have any right to tell anyone else what to do with their life? But I was wrong, Will. I shouldn't have said what I did."

"Everything you said was right on the money. I knew it even while I was reacting so strongly. I've thought the same things myself, deep in my subconscious. Robin wouldn't want me to hide away from life, to sit out here in my workshop and brood while the world carries on without me. That wasn't what she was about, what *we* were about. But even though I've thought the same thing, I can't deny that hearing it from you was tough."

"I'm so sorry."

He sighed at the misery in her voice and surrendered to the inevitable. He stepped forward and picked up her knotted fingers, feeling them tremble in his hands.

"I care about you, Julia, more than I thought I could ever care about anyone again. When I'm with you, I feel like I'm sixteen again, sitting on the beach with the prettiest girl I've ever seen. But it scares the hell out of me. I'm not ready. That's the bald, honest truth. I'm not ready and I'm afraid I don't know if I ever will be."

"That's why you're leaving?"

"I'd be lying if I said you had nothing to do with my decision to take the job with Eben. But leaving—trying something new—has been on my mind for some time. I was considering it long before you showed up again, back when you were just a distant memory of a past that sometimes feels like it should belong to someone else."

He paused, struck by the contrast of her soft, delicate hands in his fingers that were hard and roughened by years of work.

"I guess you could say you're part of the reason I'm leaving, but you're not the only reason. I need a change.

If I stay here, buried under the weight of the past, I'm afraid I'll slowly petrify like a piece of driftwood."

She took a long time to answer. Just when he was about to release her hands and step away, she clutched at his fingers with hands that still trembled.

"Would it make any difference if I...if I were the one to leave?"

He stared at her, taken aback. "Where would you go? You love your new job, Brambleberry House. Everything."

Sadness twisted across her lovely features. "I do love it here and the twins are thriving. But I have much less invested in Cannon Beach than you do. I've only been here a short time. We started over here, we can start over somewhere else."

That she would even contemplate making such a sacrifice for his sake completely astounded him.

"You can't do that for me, Julia. I would never ask of it you."

"You didn't ask. I'm offering. I hate the idea that I had anything to do with your decision to leave. I blew into town out of nowhere and ruined everything."

"You ruined nothing, Julia."

Whether he liked it or not, tenderness churned through him and he couldn't bear her distress. He lifted their joined hands and pressed his mouth to the warm skin at the back of her hand.

She shivered at his touch and he couldn't help himself. He pulled her into his arms, where she settled with a soft sigh.

"You ruined nothing," he repeated. "If anything, you made me realize I can't exist in this halflife forever. I have to move forward or I'll suffocate and right now taking this job with Eben feels like the best way to do that."

"I don't want you to leave," she murmured, her arms around his waist and her cheek against his chest.

He closed his eyes, stunned by the soft, contented peace that seemed to swirl through him. Right at this moment, he didn't want to think about leaving. Hell, he didn't want to move a muscle ever again.

They stood together for a long time, in a silence broken only by the sea outside the door and the dog's snuffly breaths as he slept.

When at last she lifted her face to his, he gave a sigh of surrender and lowered his mouth to hers.

Chapter Fourteen

His kiss was slow and gentle, like standing in a torpid stream, and it seemed to push every single thought from her head.

After their last kiss and the words they had flung at each other afterward, she had been certain she wouldn't find herself here in his arms again.

The unexpectedness of it added a poignant beauty to the moment and she leaned into him, savoring his hard strength against her.

He kissed her for long, drugging moments, until her knees were weak and her mind a pleasant muddle.

Through the soft haze that seemed to surround her, she had a vague awareness that there a subtle difference this time, something that had been missing the other times they kissed.

It took her several moments to pinpoint the change. Those other times they had kissed, he had always held part of himself back and she had sensed the reluctance underlying each touch, even when she doubted he was fully aware of it himself.

This time, that hesitancy was gone. All she tasted in his kiss was tenderness and the sweet simmer of desire.

She smiled against his mouth, unable to contain the giddy joy exploding through her.

"What's so funny?" he murmured.

"Nothing," she assured him. "Absolutely nothing. It's just…I've just missed you."

He stared at her for a long moment, his face just inches from hers, then he groaned and kissed her again. This time his mouth was wild, urgent, and she responded eagerly, pouring all the emotions in her heart into their embrace.

She was in love with him.

Even as her body stirred to life, as their mouths tangled together, as she seemed to sink into the hard strength of his arms, the truth seemed to washed over her like the storm-churned sea and she reeled under the unrelenting force of it.

He was leaving in three days and had just made it quite plain he wouldn't change his mind. Nothing but heartache awaited her. She knew it, just as she knew she was powerless to change the inevitable.

But that didn't matter. Right here, right now, she was in his arms and she couldn't waste this moment by worrying about how much she would bleed inside when he walked away.

She tightened her arms around him and he made a low sound in the back of his throat and his arms tightened around her.

"Julia," he murmured. Just her name and nothing else.

"I'm here," she whispered. "Right here."

She brushed a kiss against the skin of his jawline, savoring the scent of sawdust and hard-working male. He made a low sound in his throat that sent an answering shiver rippling down her spine.

"You're cold."

"A little," she admitted, though her reaction was more from the desire spinning wildly through her system.

"I'm sorry. I like to keep it cool out here when I'm working, especially at night to keep me awake."

He paused for a moment, his gaze a murky blue. "We could go inside," he said, with a soberness that told her exactly what he meant by the words—and how much it cost him to make the suggestion.

A hundred doubts and insecurities zinged through her head. It would be tough enough for her to handle his departure. How could she possibly let him walk away after sharing such intimacies without her heart shattering into a million pieces?

But how could she walk away *now,* when he was

offering her so much more of himself than she ever thought he would?

"Are you sure?" she asked.

He paused, taking his time before answering. "I'm not sure of anything, Julia. I only know I want you and this feels more right than anything else has in a long, long time."

"Oh, Will." She framed his face with her hands and kissed him again, pouring all her heart into the kiss.

When at last he drew back, both of them were trembling, their breathing ragged.

"I don't know if I can promise you anything," he said, his voice a low rasp in the night. "Hell, I'm almost a hundred percent certain I can't. But right now I can't bear the thought of letting you out of my arms."

"I'm not going anywhere," she said.

"Not even inside, where it's warmer and far more comfortable than my dusty workshop?"

She smiled, aware of the cold seeping through her jacket despite the heat of his embrace. "All right."

He returned her smile with one of his own and she shivered all over again at the unexpectedness of it. "I'm not going to let you freeze to death out here. Come on inside."

Conan was already standing by the door waiting for them, she saw when she managed to wrench her gaze away from Will's, as if the dog had heard and understood their complete conversation.

She shook her head at his spooky omniscience, but didn't have time to ponder it before Will was holding her hand and walking inexorably toward his house.

It had started to rain again while she was inside the workshop, a fine, cold mist that settled in her hair and made her grateful for the warmth that met them inside the house.

She hadn't been inside his home since that last summer so long ago, though she had seem glimpses of it through the window the day they had gone for ice cream, another lifetime ago.

She had the fleeting impression as she followed him inside of a roomy, comfortable place with a vaguely neglected air to it. He slept here but she had the feeling he spent as little time as possible within these walls.

Conan stopped in the kitchen and plopped down on a rug by the door but Will led her to a large family room with two adjoining deep sofas facing a giant plasma television on one wall.

"Are you still cold?" he asked. "I can start a fire. That should take the chill out of the air."

"You don't have to."

"It will only take a moment."

Without waiting for an answer, he moved to the hearth and started laying out kindling. She didn't mind, sensing he needed the time and space, just as she did, to regain a little equilibrium.

She shrugged out of her jacket and settled into one of the plump sofas, nerves careening through her.

It had been a long time for her and she hoped she wasn't unforgivably rusty. She would have been completely terrified if she didn't have the feeling he hadn't been with anyone since his wife's death.

"I imagine you have a spectacular view when it's daylight."

He gave her a rueful smile as he set a match to the kindling. "I guess. I've been looking at it every day of my life. I tend to forget how breathtaking it is. Maybe traveling a little—seeing other sights for a change—will help me appreciate what I've taken for granted all my life."

Somehow she didn't think the reminder of his imminent departure was accidental. She tried to pretend it didn't matter, even as sorrow pinched at her.

"Do you know where Eben's sending you first?"

"Outside of Boston. I'll be there for a few weeks then I guess I'm off to Italy. Quite a change for a guy who's never left the coast."

The tinder was burning brightly now so he added a heavier log. The flames quickly caught hold of it. Already, the room seemed warmer, though she wasn't sure if that was from the fire or from the nerves shimmering through her.

Will stood for a moment, watching the fire. When he seemed confident the log would burn, he turned back to her, his features impassive.

"Is something wrong?" she finally said, when the silence between them dragged on.

His sigh sounded deep, heartfelt. "You scare the hell out of me."

She tensed. "Do you want me to leave?"

"About as much as I want to take a table saw to my right arm," he admitted. "In other words, absolutely not."

Despite her nerves, she couldn't contain the laughter bubbling through her as he moved toward her and sat on the sofa beside her. He reached for her hand, but didn't seem in a rush to kiss her again.

This was lovely, she thought, sitting here gazing into the flickering firelight with a soft rain sliding against the window and his fingers tracing patterns on hers.

"I don't know if this is any consolation," she said after a moment, "but you're not the only one who's nervous. It's, uh, been a long time for me. I'd be surprised if you couldn't hear my knees knocking from there."

He gave her a careful look. "Do *you* want to leave?"

She mustered a shaky smile. "About as much as I want to *watch* you take a table saw to your right arm. In other words, absolutely not."

"Good," he murmured.

Finally he kissed her and at the delicious heat, the familiar taste and scent of him, her nerves disappeared. She was suddenly filled with the sweet assurance that this was right. She loved Will Garrett, had loved him since she was a stupid, naive girl.

She wanted this, wanted him, and even if this was all they would ever share, she wouldn't allow any regrets.

He kissed her until she was trembling, aching for more. She held him close, pouring all the emotions she couldn't verbalize into her kiss.

By the time he worked the buttons of her blouse, her head was whirling. When he pushed aside the lacy cups of her bra to touch her, she almost shattered apart right there as a torrent of sensations poured through her.

Oh, it had been far too long since she had remembered what it was to be touched with such heat and tenderness. She had forgotten this slow churn of her blood, the restless ache that seemed to fill every cell.

She arched against him, reveling in his hard strength against her curves, in his rough hands against her sensitive skin.

He groaned, low in his throat, and lowered his head to take her in his mouth. She clutched him close, her hands buried in his hair, as he teased and tasted.

His breathing was ragged when he lifted his clever, clever lips from her breast and found her mouth again while he shrugged out of his own shirt.

She couldn't help shivering as his hard strength covered her again.

"Are you still cold?" he murmured.

"Not even close," she answered, framing his face in her hands and kissing him fiercely. He responded with a groan and any tentativeness disappeared in a wild rush of heat.

In moments, they were both naked. Silhouetted in the dancing firelight, he was gorgeous, hard and muscled, ruggedly male.

"Okay, now I'm nervous again," she admitted.

"We can stop right now if you want," he said gruffly. "It might just kill me to let you out of my arms, but we don't have to go any further."

"No. I don't want to stop. Just kiss me again."

He willingly obeyed and for several long moments, only their mouths connected, then at last he pulled her close, trailing kisses from her mouth to the sensitive skin of her neck.

"Okay now?" he murmured, his body warm and hard against her.

"Oh, much, much better than okay," she breathed, her mouth tangling with his again as he pressed her back against the soft cushions of the sofa.

It was everything she might have dreamed—tender and passionate, sexy and sweet. When he filled her, she cried out, stunned at the emotions pouring through her, and she had to choke back the words of love she knew he wasn't ready to hear.

His mouth was hard and urgent on hers as he began to slowly move inside her and she lifted her hips to meet him.

Oh, she had missed this. She hadn't fully appreciated how much until right this moment.

How was she ever going to be able to go back to her solitary life?

She pushed the grim thought away, unwilling to let anything destroy the beauty of this moment.

He moved more deeply inside her and she gasped his name, feeling as breathless and shaky as the time she and Will had sneaked out to go cliff diving.

He withdrew then pushed inside her again and the contrast between the tenderness of his kiss and the wild urgency of his body sent her spinning and soaring over the edge.

With a groan, he joined her, his hands gripping hers tightly.

As they floated together back to earth, he shifted and pulled her on top of him, tugging a knit throw from the back of the sofa to cover them.

She nestled into his heat and his strength, a delicious lassitude soaking into her muscles, more content than she could ever remember being in her life.

She must have slept for a few moments, tucked into the safe shelter of his arms. When she blinked her eyes open, the grandfather clock in the hallway was tolling midnight.

Like Cinderella, she knew the spell was ending and she would have to slip away home.

She shifted her gaze to Will and found him watching her. Was he regretting what they had shared? To her frustration, she could read nothing in his veiled expression.

She sat up, reaching for her blouse as she went. "I need to go back to Brambleberry House. Sage and Anna are going to be sending a search party out after me."

He sat up and she had to force herself to look away from that broad, enticing expanse of muscles.

"Oh, somehow I doubt that. I have a feeling they know exactly where you are."

"You're probably right," she answered ruefully. "A little on the spooky side, those two."

He raised an eyebrow as he slid into his jeans. "A little?"

She smiled. "Okay. A lot. I should still go, much as I don't want to."

He was quiet for a long moment, watching out of those veiled features as she worked the buttons of her shirt.

"Julia, I can't promise you anything," he finally said.

She met his gaze, doing her best to keep the devastation at bay. "You said that earlier, and I understand, Will. I do. I don't expect anything."

He raked a hand through his hair. "I'm just so damn screwed up right now. I wish things could be otherwise. I'm just…"

She returned to him and cut his words off with a kiss, hoping he didn't taste the desperation in her kiss. This would be the one and only time for them, she knew.

He didn't have to say the words for her to accept the reality that nothing had changed. He was still leaving in a few days, and she would be left here alone with her pain.

"Will, it's okay," she lied. "My eyes were wide

open when I walked into your house. No illusions here, I promise."

"I'm so sorry." His voice was tight with genuine regret and she shook her head.

"I'm not. Not for an instant."

She drew in a breath, gathering the last vestiges of courage left inside her for what somehow she suddenly knew she had to say.

"While we're tossing our cards out on the table, I think I should tell you why I'm here."

His expression turned wary. "Why?"

She sighed. "You haven't figured it out? I'm in love with you, Will."

The words hovered between them, raw and naked, and she had to smile a little at the sudden panic in his eyes.

"I know. It was a big shock for me, too. I'm not telling you that as some kind of underhanded tactic to convince you to stay. I know that nothing I say will change your mind and, believe me, I don't expect my feelings to change your decision in any way. I just felt that you should know. I wouldn't be here with you right now if I didn't love you—it's just not the kind of thing I do."

"I think some part of me guessed as much," he admitted.

"You've been in my heart for sixteen years, Will. Through my parents' divorce, through my own difficult teen years, through the breakup of my marriage, some part of me remembered that summer with you as a wonderful, magical time. Maybe the best summer of my life. You were my first love and I've never forgotten you."

"Julia…"

She shook her head, willing herself not to cry. Not now, not yet. "You don't have to say it. I know, we were different people then. And to be honest, the place you held in my heart was precious but only a tiny, dusty little spot, a corner I peeked into once in awhile with a smile and fond memories but then quickly forgot again."

She forced a smile. "And then I came back to Cannon Beach and here you were. As I came to know you all over again, I revisited those memories and realized that the boy I fell in love with back then had become a good, honorable man. A man who takes great pride in a job well done, who talks to dogs, who cares deeply about his neighbors and is kind to children…even when they make him bleed inside."

She touched his cheek, wishing with all her heart that he was ready to accept the precious, healing gift she so wanted to offer him.

Even as she touched him, though, she didn't miss his slight, barely perceptible flinch.

"Don't. Don't love me, Julia." His voice was ragged, anguished. "I'll only hurt you."

"I know you will." She managed a wobbly smile, even though she could swear she heard the sound of her heart cracking apart. "But I'll survive it."

She kissed him again, a soft, sincere benediction, then stepped away to shrug into her jacket. "I have to go."

He didn't argue, just pulled on his own shirt and boots. "I'll walk you back."

"I have Conan. I'll be fine."

"I'll walk you back," he said firmly.

She nodded, realizing that arguing with him would only be a waste of strength and energy, two commodities she had a feeling she would be needing in the days ahead.

In truth, she didn't mind. These were probably her last few moments with him and she wanted to savor every second.

Conan was again waiting expectantly by the back door. He cocked his head, his expression quizzical. She had no idea what he could read in their expressions but he whined a little.

More than anything, she wanted to bury her face in his fur and sob but she managed to keep her composure as Will handed her an umbrella and picked up a flashlight hanging on a hook by the door.

The slow, steady rain perfectly matched her mood. She shivered a little and zipped up her jacket, then headed toward Brambleberry House.

Will didn't share the umbrella—instead, he simply pulled the hood of his Gore-Tex jacket up, which given the dark and the rain effectively obscured his features.

They walked in silence and even Conan seemed subdued, almost sad. Instead of his usual ebullient energy, he plodded along beside her with his head hanging down.

As for Will, he seemed as distant and unreachable as the Cape Meares lighthouse.

She shouldn't have told him her feelings, she thought. He already carried enough burdens. He didn't need that one, too.

He finally spoke when they approached the gates of Brambleberry House, but they weren't words she wanted to hear.

"Julia, I'm sorry," he said.

"Please don't be sorry we made love. I'm not."

"I should be. Sorry about that, I mean. But I'm not. It was…right. That's not what I meant. Mostly, I guess I'm sorry things can't be different, that we have all these years and pain between us."

She touched his cheek. "The years and the pain shaped us, Will. They're part of who we are now."

He turned his head and kissed her fingers, then pulled her into his arms once more. His kiss was tender, gentle, with an underlying note of finality to it. When he drew away, her throat ached with unshed tears.

"You're not leaving until after the wedding, are you?"

He nodded. "Sage would kill me if I missed her big day. My flight leaves the next morning."

"Well, I'll see you then, anyway. Goodbye, Will."

She had a million things she wanted to say but this

wasn't the time. None of them would make a difference anyway.

Instead, she managed one last shaky smile and tugged Conan up the stairs and into the entry, forcing herself not to look back as she heard his muffled footsteps on the sidewalk.

Anna's apartment door opened the moment Julia closed the front door behind her, and Sage and Anna both peeked their heads out into the entryway. They had changed into pajamas and she could smell the aroma of popcorn from inside the apartment.

Conan hurried inside as soon as she unclipped his leash, probably looking for any stray kernels that might have been dropped. She would have smiled if she thought she could manage it.

"So?" Sage demanded. "What happened? You were gone *forever*. Did you talk Will into staying?"

As much as she had come to love both the other women in just the few short months she had been in Cannon Beach, she couldn't bear their curiosity right now, not when her emotions had been scraped to the bone.

"No," she said, her voice low. "His mind is made up."

Sage made a sound of disgust but Anna gave her a searching, entirely perceptive look. She was suddenly aware that her hair was probably a mess and she no doubt had whisker burns on her skin.

"It's not your fault, Julia," she said after a moment. "I'm sure you tried your best."

She fought an almost hysterical urge to laugh. To hide it, she yanked off her jacket and hung it back in the closet. "He has his reasons. He didn't take the job with Eben on a whim, I can promise you that."

"That still doesn't make it right!" Sage exclaimed.

"As people who…who care about him, we owe it to Will to respect his decision, even if we don't agree with it or think it's necessarily the best one for him."

Sage looked as if she wanted to argue but Anna silenced her with a long, steady look.

"He won't change his mind?" Anna asked.

"I don't think so," Julia said.

To her surprise, though Sage was usually the demonstrative one, this time Anna was the one who pulled her into her arms for a hug. "Thanks for trying. I know it was hard for you."

You have no idea, she thought, even as Sage hugged her as well. For just a moment, Julia thought she smelled freesia and it was almost as if Abigail herself was there offering understanding and comfort.

"Don't badger him about it, okay?" she said. "It was a hard decision for him to make but I think taking the job is something he…he needs to do right now."

"Are you okay?" Anna murmured.

For one terrible moment, the sympathy in her friend's voice almost made her weep but she blinked away the tears. "Fine. Just fine. Why wouldn't I be?"

Anna didn't look convinced but to her immense

relief, she didn't push. "You look exhausted. You'd better get some rest."

She nodded with a grateful look. "It's been a long day," she agreed. "Good night."

She quickly turned and hurried up the stairs, praying she could make it inside before breaking down.

After she closed the door behind her, she checked on the twins and found them sleeping peacefully, then returned to the darkened living room. Against her will, she moved to the windows overlooking his house and saw lights on again in his workshop.

The thought of him in his solitary workshop by himself, putting the finishing touches on Maddie's spectacular dollhouse was the last straw. Tears slid down her cheeks to match the rain trickling down the window and she stood for a long time in the dark, aching and alone.

Chapter Fifteen

Three days later, he stood on the edge of the dance floor in the elegant reception room of The Sea Urchin, doing his level best not to spend the entire evening staring at Julia like the lovesick teenager he had once been.

He hadn't seen her since the night they had shared together but he was quite certain he hadn't spent more than ten minutes without thinking about her—remembering the softness of her skin, her sweet response to him, the shock that had settled in gut when she told him she loved him.

Just now she was dancing with her son, laughing as she tried to show him the steps of the fox-trot. She looked bright and vibrant and beautiful in a lovely, flowing green dress that matched her eyes. Despite her apparent enjoyment in the evening, he was almost certain he had caught a certain sadness in her eyes whenever their gazes happened to collide, and his heart ached, knowing he had put it there.

He couldn't stay much longer. He was leaving in the morning and still had work to do packing and closing up his house for an indefinite time. Beyond that, it hurt more than he ever would have dreamed to keep his distance from Julia, to stand on the sidelines and watch her, knowing he could never have her.

He needed to at least talk to Sage before he escaped, he knew. When the music ended and she returned to the edge of the dance floor on the arm of ancient Mr. Delarosa, one of Abigail's old friends, he hurried to claim her before anyone else.

"Have any dances left for an old friend?"

Surprise flickered in her eyes, then she gave him a brilliant smile. "Of course!"

He wasn't much of a dancer but he did his best, grateful at least that it was another slow song and he wasn't going to have to make an idiot out of himself by trying to shake and groove.

"You make a stunning bride, kiddo," he said when they fell into a rhythm. "Who ever would have believed it?"

He gave an exaggerated wince when she punched him lightly in the shoulder.

"You know I'm teasing," he said, squeezing the fingers he held. "I'm thrilled for you and Eben, Sage. I really am. You're a beautiful bride and it was a beautiful ceremony."

"It was, wasn't it? I only wish Abigail could have been here."

"I don't doubt she was, in her own way."

She smiled, as he intended. "I think you're probably right. I was quite sure I smelled freesia at least once while Eben and I were exchanging our vows."

"I'm glad the weather held for you." It had been a gorgeous, sunny day, warm and lovely, a rarity on the coast for October.

"I thought for sure we were going to have to move everything inside for the ceremony but the weather couldn't have been more perfect."

"That's because Mother Nature knows she owes you big-time for all your do-gooder, save-the-world efforts. She wouldn't dare ruin your big day with rain."

She laughed softly then sobered quickly. "I forgot, I'm not supposed to be speaking to you. I'm still mad at you."

"Don't start, Sage. We've been over this. I'm going. But it's not forever—I'll be back."

"It won't be the same."

"Nothing will. Look at you, Mrs. Spencer. You're moving to San Francisco with Eben and Chloe. Things change, Sage."

"I'm going to miss you, darn it. You're the big,

annoying, overprotective brother I've always wanted, Will."

He was more touched than he would dare admit. "And since the day you moved in to Brambleberry House, you've been like a bratty little sister to me, always sure you know what's best for everyone."

She made a harumph kind of sound. "That's because I do. For instance, I am quite certain you're making a huge mistake to leave Cannon Beach and a certain resident of Brambleberry House who shall remain nameless."

"Who? Conan?"

She smacked his shoulder again. "You know who I mean. Julia."

He shook his head. "Leave it alone, Sage."

"I won't." She stuck her chin out with a stubbornness he should have expected, knowing Sage. "If Abigail were here, she would tell you the exact same thing. You can't lie to me, you have feelings for Julia, don't you?"

"None of your business. This is a great band, by the way. Where did you find them?"

"I didn't, Jade Wu did. You know perfectly well she handled all the wedding details. And I won't let you change the subject. What kind of idiot walks away from a woman as fabulous as Julia, who just happens to be crazy about him?"

"I'm going to leave you right here in the middle of the dance floor if you don't back off," he warned her.

Though he spoke amicably enough, he put enough steel in his voice that he hoped she got the message.

She gave him a piercing look and then her gaze suddenly softened. "You're as miserable as she is! You know you are."

He shifted his gaze to Julia, who was dancing and smiling with the owner of the bike shop—who just happened to be the biggest player in town.

"She doesn't look miserable to me."

They were several couples away from them on the dance floor, but just at that moment, her partner swung her around so she was facing him. They made eye contact and for one sizzling moment, it was as if they were alone in the room.

He caught his breath, snared by those deep green eyes for a long moment, until her partner turned her again.

"She does a pretty good job of hiding it, but she is," Sage said.

She paused, then met his gaze. "Did I ever tell you how I almost lost Eben and Chloe because I was too afraid of being hurt to let them inside my heart?"

"I don't think you did," he said stiffly.

"It's a long story but look at the happy ending, just because I decided Eben's love was worth far more to me than my pride. You're the most courageous man I know, Will. You've walked through hell these last few years. I know that, know that you've endured more than anyone should have to—a pain that most of us probably couldn't even guess at. Don't you think you've been through enough? You deserve happiness. Do you really think you're going to find it traveling around the world, leaving behind your home and everyone who loves you?"

"I don't know," he said, more struck by her words than he cared to admit. "But I'm going anyway. This is your wedding day. I don't want to fight with you about this. I appreciate your concern for me, but everything will be fine."

She sighed and probably would have said more but Eben came up behind them at that moment.

"What does a guy have to do to get a dance with his bride?"

"Just ask," Will said. "She's all yours."

He kissed Sage on the cheek and released her. "Thanks for the dance and the advice," he said. "Congratulations again to both of you."

Much as he loved her, he was relieved to walk away and leave her to Eben. He didn't need more of her lectures about how he was making a mistake to leave or her not-so-subtle hints about Julia.

What he needed was to get out of here, and soon. He couldn't take much more.

He made it almost to the door when he felt a sharp tug on his jacket. He turned around and found Maddie Blair standing beside him wearing a frilly blue party dress and a blazing smile.

His heart caught just a little but he probed around and

realized he no longer had the piercing pain he used to whenever he saw Julia's dark-haired daughter.

"Hi," she said.

He forced himself to smile back. "Hi yourself."

"I had to tell you how much I love, love, *love* my dollhouse. It's the best dollhouse in the whole world! Thank you so much!"

"I'm glad you like it."

"Did you know it has a doorbell that really works? And it even has a secret closet in the bedroom that you open a special way."

"I believe I did know that."

He had finally finished the dollhouse late into the night two days before and had dropped it off at Brambleberry House, leaving it covered with a tarp on the porch for Julia to find. He knew it was cowardly to drop it off in the middle of the night. He should have picked a time when he could help carry it up the stairs for her, but he hadn't been able to face her.

"I would like to dance with you," Maddie announced, leaving him no room for arguments.

"Um, sure," he said, not knowing how to wiggle out of it. "I'd like that."

It wasn't even a lie, he realized to his surprise. He held out his arm in a formal kind of gesture and she grinned and slipped her hand into the crook of his elbow. Together they worked their way through the crowd to the dance floor.

While they danced, Maddie kept up an endless stream of conversation during the dance—about her dolls, about how she was going to go visit Chloe in San Francisco some time, about some mischief her brother had been up to.

He listened to her light chatter while the music poured around him, making appropriate comments whenever she stopped to take a breath.

"You're the best dancer I've danced with tonight," she said when the song was almost at an end. "Simon stepped on my toes a million times and I think he even broke one. And Chloe's dad wouldn't stop looking at Sage the whole time we danced. I think that's rude, don't you, even if they did just get married. Grown-ups are weird."

Will couldn't help it, he looked down at Maddie's animated little face and laughed out loud.

"You have a nice laugh," she observed, watching him through her wise little eyes that had endured too much. "I like it."

"Thanks," he answered, a little taken aback.

"You know what?" she whispered, as if confiding state secrets, and he had to bend his head a little lower to hear her, until their faces were almost touching.

"What?" he whispered back.

"I like you, too." She smiled at him, then before he realized what she intended, she stood on her tiptoes and kissed his cheek.

He stared at her as her words seemed to curl through

him, squeezing the air from his lungs and sending all the careful barriers he thought he had built around his heart tumbling with one big, hard shove.

"Thanks," he finally said around the golf ball-size lump in his throat. "I, uh, like you, too."

It wasn't quite true, he realized with shock. His feelings for this little girl and her brother ran deeper than simple affection.

He had tried so hard to keep them all at bay but somehow when he wasn't looking, Julia's twins had sneaked into his heart. He cared about them—Simon, with his inquisitive mind and his eagerness to please, and Maddie with her unrelenting courage and the simple joy she seized from life.

How the hell had he let such a thing happen? He thought he had been so careful around them to keep his distance but something had gone terribly wrong.

He remembered Maddie offering to eat her ice cream slowly so he could have a taste if he wanted, Simon talking about baseball and inviting him to watch a Mariners' game, budding hero worship in his eyes.

He loved Julia's children.

Just as he loved their mother.

He stopped stockstill on the dance floor. It *couldn't* be true. It couldn't. His gaze found Julia, standing at the refreshment table talking to Anna. She looked graceful and lovely. When she felt his gaze, she turned and gave him a tentative smile and he suddenly wanted nothing more than he wanted to yank her into his arms and carry her out of here.

"Are you okay, Mr. Garrett?" Maddie asked.

"I...yes. Thank you for the dance," he said, his voice stiff.

"You're welcome. Will you come play Barbies with me sometime?"

He had to get out of there, right now. The noise and the crowd were pressing in on him, suffocating him.

"Maybe. I'll see you later, okay?"

She nodded and smiled, then slipped away. On his way out the door, his gaze caught Julia's one more time and he hoped to hell the shock of his newfound feelings didn't show in his expression.

She gave him another tentative smile, which he acknowledged with a jerky nod, then he slipped out the door.

He climbed into his pickup in a kind of daze and pulled out of The Sea Urchin's parking lot in the pale twilight, not knowing where he was heading, only that he had to get away. He thought he was driving aimlessly, following the curve of the ocean, but before he quite realized it, he found himself at the small cemetery at twilight, just as the sunset turned the waves a soft, pale blue.

He parked outside the gates, knowing he didn't have long since the cemetery was supposed to be closed after dark. Leaves crunched underfoot as he followed the familiar path, listening to the quiet reverence of the place.

He stopped at his father's grave first, under the spreading boughs of a huge, majestic oak tree. It was a fitting resting place for a man who could work such magic with his hands and a piece of wood. He stopped, head bowed, remembering the many lessons he had learned from his father. Work hard, play hard, cherish your family.

Not a bad mantra for a man to follow.

After long moments, he let out a breath and walked over a small hill to Abigail's grave, decorated with many tokens of affection. Sage had left her a wedding invitation, he saw, and a flower from her bouquet, and Will couldn't help smiling.

He saved the toughest for last. With emotion churning through him, he followed the trail around another curve, almost to the edge by the fence, where two simple headstones marked Robin and Cara's graves.

He hadn't been here in a few months, he realized with some shock. Right after the accident he used to come here every day, sometimes twice a day. He had hated it, but he had come. Those visits had dwindled but he had always tried to come at least once a week to bring his wife whatever flowers were in season.

Like Abigail, Robin had loved flowers.

Guilt coursed through him as he realized how he had neglected his responsibilities.

He rounded the last corner and there they were, silhouetted in the dying sun. Two simple markers—Robin

Cramer Garrett, beloved wife. Cara Robin Garrett, cherished daughter.

Emotions clogged his throat. Oh, he missed them. He walked closer, then he blinked in shock, certain the dusky twilight must be playing tricks with his eyesight.

A few weeks after the accident, Abigail had asked him if she could plant a rosebush between Robin and Cara's graves. He had been wild with grief, inconsolable, and wouldn't have cared whether she planted a whole damn flower garden, so he had given his consent.

He hadn't paid it much attention, other than to note a few times in the summer that if she had still been alive, Abigail would have been devastated to know she must have planted a sterile bush. He hadn't seen a single bloom on it in two years.

Now, though, as he stood in the cool October air, he stared in shock at the rosebush. It was covered in flowers—hundreds of them, in a rich, vibrant yellow.

This couldn't be right. He didn't know a hell of a lot about horticulture but he was fairly certain roses bloomed in summer. It was mid-October now, and had been colder than usual the last few weeks, rainy and dank.

It made absolutely no sense but he couldn't ignore the evidence in front of him. Abigail's roses were sending their lush, sweet fragrance into the air, stirring gently in a soft breeze.

Let go, Will. Life moves on.

He could almost swear he heard Abigail's words on the breeze, her voice as brisk and no-nonsense as always.

He sank down onto the wooden bench he had built and stared at the flower-heavy boughs, softly caressing the marble markers.

Let go.

His breathing ragged, he gazed at the flowers, stunned by the emotion pouring through him like a cleansing, healing rainstorm, something he hadn't known since his family was taken from him with such sudden cruelty.

Hope.

It was hope.

These roses seemed a perfect symbol of it, a precious gift Abigail had left behind just for him, as if she knew that somehow he would need to see those blossoms at exactly this moment in his life to remind him of things he had lost along the way.

Hope, faith. Love.

Life moves on.

Whether he was ready for it or not, he loved Julia Blair and her children. They had showed him that his life was not over, that if he could only find the courage, his future didn't have to be this grim, empty existence.

She had roared back into his life like a hurricane, blowing away all the shadows and darkness, the bone-deep misery that had been his companion for two years.

He couldn't say the idea of loving her and her kids still didn't scare the hell out of him. He had already lost more than he could bear. But the idea of living without them—of going back to his gray and cheerless life—scared him more.

He sat on the bench for a long time while the cemetery darkened and the roses danced and swayed in the breeze, surrounding him with their sweet perfume.

When at last he stood up, his cheeks were wet but his heart felt a million times lighter. He headed for the cemetery gates, with only one destination in mind.

Chapter Sixteen

"Mama, I just love weddings." Though she was drooping with fatigue, Maddie's eyes were bright as Julia helped her out of her organza dress.

"It was lovely, wasn't it?"

"Sage was so pretty in her dress. She looked like an angel. And Chloe did a good job throwing the flower petals, didn't she? She didn't even look one bit nervous!"

Julia smiled at Maddie's enthusiasm. "She was the best flower girl I've ever seen."

"Do you think when you get married, I could wear a dress like Chloe's and throw flower petals, too?"

She winced, not at all sure how to answer. "Um, honey, I've already been married, to your dad," she finally said.

"But you could get married again, couldn't you? Chloe said you could because her dad was already married before, too, to her mom. Then her mom died just like Daddy and now her dad is married again to Sage."

Julia forced a smile. "Isn't it lucky he found Sage?"

She, on the other hand, had given her heart to Will Garrett, wholly and completely, and somehow she knew she would never be able to love anyone else. Will wasn't ready for it. For all she knew, he would *never* be ready. If Will couldn't bring himself to love her back, she was afraid she would spend the rest of her life alone.

But she wasn't about to confide her heartache to her daughter. "You need to get to sleep, kiddo. It's been a big day and I know you're tired. Simon's already in his bed, sound asleep."

She helped Maddie into her nightgown and was tucking her under the covers when Maddie touched her hand.

"Mama, I think you should marry Mr. Garrett."

Julia nearly tripped over Maddie's slippers in her astonishment. "Wh…why would you say that?"

"Well, lots of reasons. He smells nice and I just love the dollhouse he made me."

Not the worst reasons for a seven-year-old girl to come up with to marry a man, she supposed.

"And maybe if you married him, he wouldn't be so sad all the time. You make him smile, Mama. I know you do."

Tears burned in her eyelids at Maddie's confident statement and she knelt down to fold her daughter into her arms.

"Go to sleep, pumpkin," she said through the emotions clogging her throat. "I'll see you in the morning."

She turned off the light and closed her door, then moved to Simon's room to check on him. He was sleeping soundly, his blankets already a tangle at his waist. She tucked them back over his shoulders then returned to the living room, lit only by a small lamp next to her Stickley rocking chair.

Though she tried to fight the impulse, she finally gave in and moved to the window overlooking Will's house. No lights were on there, she saw. Was he asleep already?

He was leaving in the morning. Maybe he intended to get a solid night's rest for traveling across the country.

The emotions Maddie had stirred in her finally broke free and she felt tears trickling down her cheeks. He hadn't said a word to her all day. She had felt his gaze several times, both during the ceremony and then after at the reception, but he hadn't approached her.

After his dance with Maddie, she had intended to track him down—if only to tell him goodbye before he left for his new job—but he had rushed out of The Sea Urchin so fast she hadn't had the chance.

She didn't need a pile of two-by-fours to fall on her head to figure out he didn't want to talk to her again.

She swiped at her tears with her palm. He hadn't even left town yet and she already missed him like crazy. Despite her determined claims to him that she wouldn't regret making love, she couldn't deny that the tender intimacy they had shared had only ratcheted up her pain to a near-unbearable level.

Sage's joy today had only served to reinforce to Julia that she was unlikely ever to know that kind of happiness with Will. He might have opened up his emotions to her a few nights ago but now they were as tightly locked and shoved away as they had been since she returned to town. If she needed proof, she only had to look at the careful distance he maintained at the wedding.

What a strange journey she had traveled since making the decision to return to Cannon Beach. She never would have guessed when she took that teaching job several months ago that she would find love and heartbreak all in one convenient package.

He was leaving in the morning and she could do nothing to stop him.

She sobbed, just a little, then the sound caught in her throat when she suddenly thought she smelled freesia.

"Oh, Abigail," she murmured. "I wish you were here to tell me what to do, how I can reach Will. I don't think I can bear this."

Silence met her impassioned plea, but an instant later she jumped a mile when she felt something wet brush her hand.

"Conan! You scared the life out of me! Where were you?"

The dog had followed her and the twins upstairs when

they returned to Brambleberry House from the wedding, apparently needing company since Anna was still busy cleaning up at the reception and Sage and Eben were staying at The Sea Urchin for the night until they left for their honeymoon in the Galapagos in the morning.

He must have gone into her room to lie down, since she hadn't seen him when she came out of Simon's room and had forgotten he was even there. Still, she had to admit she was grateful for the company. The dog leaned against her leg, offering his own unique kind of support and sympathy.

"Thanks," she whispered, as they sat together in her dim apartment looking out at the lights of town.

But his steady comfort didn't last long. After a moment, his ears pricked up and he suddenly barked and rushed for the door, his tail wagging.

She sighed. "You want to go out *again?* We let you out when we came home!"

He whined a little and watched her out of those curiously intelligent eyes. With a sigh, she abandoned any fleeting hope she might have briefly entertained about sinking into a hot bubble bath to soak away her misery, for a while anyway.

"All right, you crazy dog. Just let me find some shoes first."

She had changed after the reception into worn jeans and her oldest, most comfortable sweater. Now she grabbed tennis shoes and headed down the stairs.

The moment she opened the outside door, Conan rocketed down the porch steps and toward the front gate, then disappeared from sight.

Oh rats. She forgot to check that the gate was still closed. Conan usually stuck close to home, preferring his own territory, but if he smelled a cat anywhere in the vicinity, all bets were off.

What was she supposed to do now? No one else was home, the twins were sleeping upstairs and the dog was loose. She couldn't let him wander free, though.

"Conan," she called. "Get back here."

He barked from what sounded like just the other side of the ironwork fence, but she couldn't see him in the darkness.

"Here, boy. Come on."

He didn't respond to the command and with a sigh, she headed down the sidewalk, hoping he wasn't in the mood for a playful game of tag. She wasn't at all in the mood to chase him.

"Come on, Conan. It's cold." She walked through the gate, then froze when she saw in the moonlight just why the dog hadn't answered her summons.

He was busy greeting a man who stood silent and watchful on the other side of the fence.

Will.

She stared at him, stunned to find him here, tonight, and wondering if she had left any evidence of the tears she had just shed for him. All those emotions just under the surface threatened to break through again—sorrow and regret, doubt, sadness.

Love.

Especially love.

She wanted to go to him, throw her arms around his waist and beg him not to leave.

"I didn't see you there," she said instead, hoping her emotional tumult didn't show up in her voice.

He said nothing, just continued to pet the dog and watch her. She walked a little closer.

"Is everything okay?"

"No." His voice sounded hoarse, ragged. "I don't think it is."

He stepped closer to her, so near she could smell the scent of his aftershave, sexy and male. Her heart, already pounding hard since the instant she saw him standing in the darkness, picked up a pace.

"What is it?"

He was quiet for a long time—so long she was beginning to worry something was seriously wrong. Finally, to her immense shock he reached out and grasped her fingers and pulled her even closer.

"I had to come. Had to see you."

"Why?"

His slow sigh stirred her hair. "I love you, Julia."

"Wh-what did you say?" She jerked her hand away and scrambled back. Her heartbeat accelerated and she couldn't seem to catch her breath as shock rippled through her.

He raked a hand through his hair. "I didn't mean to just blurt it out like that. I must sound like an idiot."

"I'm...I'm sorry. You don't sound like an idiot. I just...I wasn't expecting that. You're leaving tomorrow. Aren't you leaving?"

A tiny flutter of joy started in her heart but she was afraid to let it free, afraid he would only crush it and leave her feeling worse than ever.

"Yes. I'm leaving."

She expected his words but they still scored her heart. He said he loved her, but he was leaving anyway?

"I wish I didn't have to go but I gave my word to Eben and I'm committed, at least for a few weeks, until he can find someone else to take my place."

He reached for her hand again and she could feel her fingers trembling in his hard, callused palm. "And then I'd like to come back. To Cannon Beach and to you."

While she was still reeling from his words, he paused, then touched her cheek softly. "You were so right about everything you've said to me. I need to move forward, to give myself the freedom to taste all life has to offer again. It's time. I've known it's time, but I've been so afraid. That's a tough thing for a man to admit, but it's the truth. I was afraid to let myself love you, afraid I was somehow...betraying Robin and Cara by all the feelings I was starting to have for you."

She squeezed his fingers. "Oh, Will. You'll never stop loving them. I would never ask that of you. That's exactly the way it should be. But the heart is a magical thing.

Abigail taught me that. When you're ready, when you need it to, it can miraculously expand to make room."

He studied her for a long moment and then suddenly he smiled. Only when she saw his mouth tilt, saw the genuine happiness in his expression, did she realize he truly meant what he said. *He loved her.* She still couldn't quite absorb it, but his eyes in the soft moonlight were free of any lingering grief and sorrow.

He loved her.

He cupped his hands around her face and kissed her then, soft and gentle in the cool October air. She wrapped her arms around his waist as a sweet, cleansing joy exploded through her.

"My heart has made room for you, Julia. For you and your beautiful children. How could it help but find a place? You already had your own corner there sixteen years ago. I think some part of me was just waiting for you to return and move back in."

His mouth found hers again, and in his kiss she tasted joy and healing and the promise of a sweet, beautiful future.

Not far away, a huge mongrel dog sat on his haunches watching them both with satisfaction in his eyes while the soft, flowery scent of freesia floated in the autumn air.

* * * * *

HARLEQUIN®

Super Romance®

Texas Hold 'Em

When it comes to love, the stakes are high

Sixteen years ago, Luke Chisum dated
Becky Parker on a dare…before going
on to break her heart. Now the former
River Bluff daredevil is back, rekindling
desire and tempting Becky to pick up
where they left off. But this time she has
to resist or Luke could discover the secret
she's kept locked away all these years.…

Look for

TEXAS BLUFF

by Linda Warren

#1470

*Available February 2008
wherever you buy books.*

The best in Western romance from
New York Times #1 bestselling author

DEBBIE MACOMBER

When Taylor Manning accepts a teaching job in Cougar Point,
Montana, she discovers that life there is very different from
life in Seattle. So are the men! She soon notices a handsome,
opinionated, stubborn rancher named Russ Palmer…and he
notices her. After only a few months, Taylor's certain of one
thing: she'd love to be The Cowboy's Lady.

The first day Christy Manning visits her sister, Taylor,
she meets Sheriff Cody Franklin. And to Christy's shock—
and Cody's—they're immediately attracted to each other.
There's a problem, though. Christy's engaged to someone
else. So what's the solution? See what happens when
The Sheriff Takes a Wife…

The Manning Sisters

"Macomber has a gift for evoking the emotions that are at
the heart of the genre's popularity."—*Publishers Weekly*

Available the first week of January 2008 wherever paperbacks are sold!

MIRA®

MDM2530

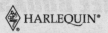

REQUEST YOUR FREE BOOKS!

2 FREE NOVELS PLUS 2 FREE GIFTS!

V TM *Silhouette*®

SPECIAL EDITION®

Life, Love and Family!

YES! Please send me 2 FREE Silhouette Special Edition® novels and my 2 FREE gifts. After receiving them, if I don't wish to receive any more books, I can return the shipping statement marked "cancel." If I don't cancel, I will receive 6 brand-new novels every month and be billed just $4.24 per book in the U.S., or $4.99 per book in Canada, plus 25¢ shipping and handling per book and applicable taxes, if any*. That's a savings of at least 15% off the cover price! I understand that accepting the 2 free books and gifts places me under no obligation to buy anything. I can always return a shipment and cancel at any time. Even if I never buy another book from Silhouette, the two free books and gifts are mine to keep forever.   235 SDN EEYU   335 SDN EEY6

Name	(PLEASE PRINT)

Address	Apt.

City	State/Prov.	Zip/Postal Code

Signature (if under 18, a parent or guardian must sign)

Mail to the **Silhouette Reader Service**™:
IN U.S.A.: P.O. Box 1867, Buffalo, NY 14240-1867
IN CANADA: P.O. Box 609, Fort Erie, Ontario L2A 5X3

Not valid to current Silhouette Special Edition subscribers.

Want to try two free books from another line?
Call 1-800-873-8635 or visit www.morefreebooks.com.

* Terms and prices subject to change without notice. NY residents add applicable sales tax. Canadian residents will be charged applicable provincial taxes and GST. This offer is limited to one order per household. All orders subject to approval. Credit or debit balances in a customer's account(s) may be offset by any other outstanding balance owed by or to the customer. Please allow 4 to 6 weeks for delivery.

Your Privacy: Silhouette is committed to protecting your privacy. Our Privacy Policy is available online at www.eHarlequin.com or upon request from the Reader Service. From time to time we make our lists of customers available to reputable firms who may have a product or service of interest to you. If you would prefer we not share your name and address, please check here. ☐

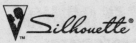
COMING NEXT MONTH